Wall Of Peril

The Princess Maura Tales
Saga of the de Magela Family

Book Two

Abigail Keam

Worker Bee Press

Worker Bee Press
P.O. Box 485
Nicholasville, KY 40340

Acknowledgements

Thanks to my editors,
Patti DeYoung and Jacy Mackin

Artwork by Karin Claesson
www.sweediesart.deviantart.com

Special thanks to
Peter Keam and Betsy Meredith

Book Jacket by Peter Keam
Author's photograph by Peter Keam

Also by Author

The Josiah Reynolds Mystery Series
Death By A HoneyBee I
Death By Drowning II
Death By Bridle III
Death By Bourbon IV
Death By Lotto V
Death By Chocolate VI
Death By Haunting VII
Death By Derby VIII
Death By Design IX
Death By Malice X

The Princess Maura Epic Fantasy Tales
Wall Of Doom I
Wall Of Peril II
Wall Of Glory III
Wall Of Conquest IV
Wall Of Victory V

Last Chance For Love Series
The Last Chance Motel I
Gasping For Air II
The Siren's Call III
Hard Landing IV
The Mermaid's Carol V

Audio Books
The Last Chance Motel
Gasping For Air

To Neil Chethik,
You made my dreams come true

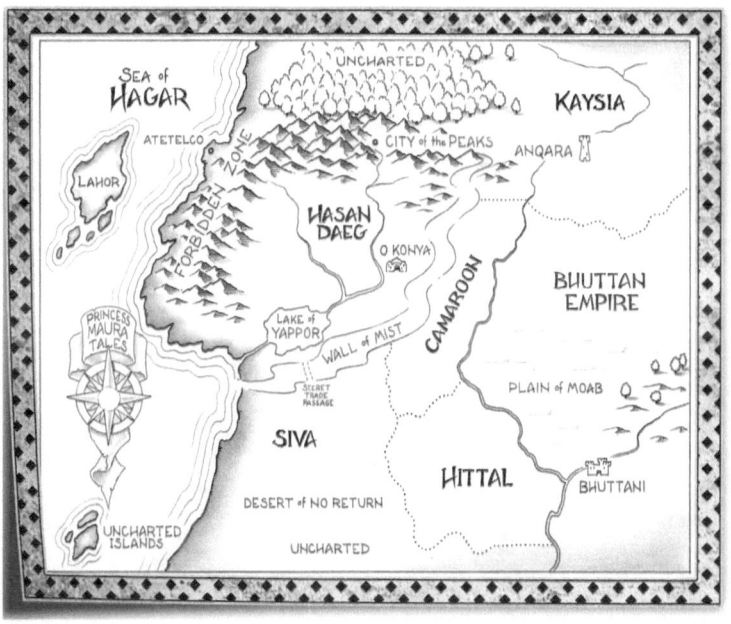

The Princess Maura Series Glossary

Abisola de Magela (character) – ninth queen of Hasan Daeg and mother of Princess Maura

Aga (character) – term for king of the Bhuttanians

Alexanee (character) – top Bhuttanian general, illegitimate older brother of Dorak

Anqara (place) – ancient cultural and banking city located in country of Kaysia

Atetelco (place) – former capital of the Dinii located in the Forbidden Zone

Beca (character) – Princess Maura's pony

Benzar (character) – gray male hawk from secret society that protects Maura

Bes Amon Ptah (character) – Moab prince hiding under the name of Timon Ben Ibin Moab

Bhutta (character) – female deity of Bhuttanians, wife of Bhuttu

Bhuttan (place) – country ruled by Zoar and his son, Dorak

Bhuttani (place) – capital of Bhuttan

Bhuttanians (characters) – nomadic people who rose to world domination under the leadership of Zoar

Bhuttu (character) – male deity of Bhuttanians whose worship calls for the sacrifice of one's life

Bilboa (characters) – race of people with red eyes who see in the dark

Bird People (characters) – the Dinii who were Overlords of Kaseri

Black Cacodemon (character) – evil wizard of Bhuttu

Blue and gold – royal colors of the Hasan Daegians

Blue Queen (character) – nickname for Maura

Boaeps – small domesticated hopping animals

Borax (both plural and singular) – bison-like animals with sharp blades down their spines

Camaroon (place) – borders Hasan Daeg, absorbed by Bhuttanian Empire

Cappet (character) – petty thief, controls eastern part of Bhuttani

Caromate plant – provides hypnotic mist when leaves are pressed

Chaun Maaun (character) – prince of the Dinii and son of the Dinii Empress Gitar

City of the Peaks (place) – city on top of highest peak in Hasan Daeg where the Dinii live

Colla – nuts from the colla tree, brewed for teas

de Magela (characters) – name of ruling family in Hasan Daeg

Dini (character) – singular of Dinii

Dinii (characters) – ancient rulers of Kaseri, formerly called Overlords, human-like beings covered with feathers who fly

Divigi (character) – spiritual leader of the Dinii and uncle to Empress Gitar

Dorak (character) – son of Zoar, aga of the Bhuttanians

Duchy of Enos (place) – estate passed down through the family of Iasos, husband of Queen Abisola

Duke Enos (character) – father of Iasos

Dyanna (character) – princess born to Maura and Dorak

Everlynd (character) – duchess of Enos and sister of Prince Consort Iasos

Forbidden Zone (place) – former home of the Dinii, cursed by both the Dinii and Hasan Daegians

Gitar (character) – empress of the Dinii and Hasan Daegians

Gootee – duck-like animal

Great Death – name given to the practice of Hasan Daegian queens willing themselves to die

Great Mother – title of respect for older women or those in power, including queens of Hasan Daeg

Hasan Daeg (place) – peaceful agricultural country ruled by the Dinii and the de Magela family

Hasan Daegian betrothal (custom) – woman asks man permission to court by kissing man's hand; if man wishes to engage, he returns the kiss; woman gives man flowers

Hasan Daegians (characters) – peaceful agricultural people who were former slaves of the Dinii

Hetmaan (character) – Bhuttanian term for Spymaster KiKu

Hittal (place) – country conquered by Zoar, land of KiKu the Hetmaan

House of Magi (place) – ancient residence of scholars in Anqara

Iasos (character) – consort of Queen Abisola and father of Princess Maura

Iegani (character) – uncle to Empress Gitar, spiritual advisor to the Dinii, and founder of secret society that protects Princess Maura

Jezra (character) – first wife to Dorak, mother of his first child

Jon (character) – minister to Governor Petenptope of the northern Hasan Daegian state of Kinton

Kaseri (place) – name of the planet

Kaysia (place) – land in which Anqara was located

KiKu (character) – Zoar's Hetmaan, former prince of Hittal who becomes a double spy

KiKusan (character) – daughter of Kiku and concubine of Zoar

Kimtimee (character) – Queen Abisola's highest-ranking general

Kinton (place) – northern region of Hasan Daeg

Kittum (place) – country to the east of Hasan Daeg which has a treaty with Bhuttan

Knoxel (character) – magician who was mentor to Zedek

Land of the Setting Sun (place) – romantic name given to Hasan Daeg by the Bhuttanians

Lahor (place) – former island home of the Lahorians

Lahorians (characters) – originally from Lahor and ancient enemies of the Dinii

Mamora (character) – first wife of Zoar and sister of KiKu

Maura (character) – tenth ruler of Hasan Daeg, daughter of Queen Abisola and Consort Iasos

Meagan of Skujpor (character) – healer to the royal house of de Magela and member of the House of Magi

Mehmet (character) – high priestess of the House of Magi

Mekonia (character) – nature goddess of the Hasan Daegians

MeNe (character) – Yesemek's first lieutenant

Mikkotto (character) – Hasan Daegian baroness who becomes a traitor and joins with Zoar

Mingo tree – tree with large, flat limbs that is treasured for its endurance, beauty, and strength

Mother Bogazkoy/Royal Bogazkoy – intelligent, self-aware plants that have a special relationship with Hasan Daegian rulers

Nani (character) – adopted granddaughter of Lady Sari

Noabini (character) – Mehmet's assistant who becomes high priestess of the House of Magi

O Konya (place) – capital of Hasan Daeg

Onxor (character) – priest of Bhuttu

Petenptope (character) – governor of the northern Hasan Daegian province of Kinton

Plain of Moab (place) – traditional home of nomadic people

Prosperot (character) – one of two top Bhuttanian generals, along with Alexanee

Qatou (place) – Hasan Daegian city

Rakel (character) – Lahorian woman who helps Princess Maura

Red – royal color of the Bhuttanians

Renna (character) – daughter of Riza

Riza (character) – scion from oldest noble family in Hasan Daeg

Rooshars – rare marsh flower

Rosalind (character) – first queen of Hasan Daeg

Royal Bogazkoy – plant offspring of the Mother Bogazkoy

Rubank (character) – consul to Queen Abisola and then to Queen Maura

Sari (character) – Hasan Daegian nurse to Queen Maura/Queen Abisola and grandmother of Mikkotto and Nani

Shaybar – Bhuttanian drink of boiled water or milk mixed with an equal portion of borax blood

Sinjo – rare berry made into wine that stimulates feelings of pleasure

Siva (place) – desert country south of Hasan Daeg

Sivans (characters) – merchant desert people

Sumsumitoyo (character) – family name of Mikkotto and Sari

Tarsus (character) – gray male hawk Dini who belongs to secret society that protects Maura

Tnpothar (character) – Zoar's father

Toppo (character) – red female hawk Dini, belongs to the secret society that protects Maura

Tsnsuni – ritualistic national prayer for the Hasan Daegian queen

Uultepes – mythical animals that are the symbol of Hasan Daegian royalty

Water Orbs – Lahorian mechanical devices constructed for transportation

Wise Ones (character) – title for the Lahorians

Yagomba tree – largest hardwood tree on Kaseri, has mystical powers

Yappor (place) – sacred lake of the Hasan Daegians and thought to be home of their goddess, Mekonia; home to the Lahorians

Yesemek (character) – commander-in-chief of the Dinii and wife to Iegani

Yeti (character) – red female hawk Dini, belongs to secret society that protects Maura

Yubuto (character) – sacrificed son of Mikkotto

Zedek (character) – Black Cacodemon's given name

Zoar (character) – aga (king) of the Bhuttanians

Wall of Peril

Preface

The peaceful country of Hasan Daeg has not fought a war in over six hundred years. But the winds of conflict blow across their hidden borders.

From the eastern plains of Bhuttan, comes a nomadic horse tribe. The Bhuttanians, bent on assimilating all countries into their empire, are causing the world to fall into chaos.

Only the Hasan Daegians and the Dinii stand between them and world domination, and they pin their hopes on Princess Maura to save them.

After the Hasan Daegians and the Dinii wage a brilliant first battle against the Bhuttanians, Dorak, son of Aga Zoar, calls upon a dark wizard to use black magic.

Helpless against this evil, the Dinii and Hasan Daegians are forced to retreat, but before they can regroup, the Bhuttanians overtake Hasan Daeg.

As Maura desperately tries to save her parents, Queen Abisola and Consort Iasos, from capitulating to

Dorak, Baroness Mikkotto enters the fray and deals a deathblow.

And so our story continues with Baroness Mikkotto.

Prologue

Baroness Mikkotto pushed open the doors.

Through the majestic brass doors of the royal palace, its gleaming white walls and floors now stained with blood, she entered cautiously. Bodies of Hasan Daegians and the Dinii were strewn throughout the hall and staircase. Mikkotto ordered her guards to move the corpses out of her way, fearful that a soldier might play dead and stab her as she stepped over. Soldiers who moaned when moved were quickly dispatched by an axe.

The horrible chunking noise of the metal striking bone did not bother Mikkotto, who calmly studied the carnage. Between the death throes of her countrywomen, Mikkotto listened for commotion in the palace. She knew Abisola and Iasos were nearby. Did they go downstairs into the bowels of the royal stronghold? Or were they on the rooftop waiting for extraction by the surviving Dinii?

It didn't matter. Mikkotto had placed guards at every exit point. She was searching for the royal family, and she must reach them before Dorak.

Dorak! She had to hand it to him. He had made an inspired play by recalling the Black Cacodemon and using magic to invade Hasan Daeg. By manipulating the wizard's powers, Dorak was able to conquer Hasan Daeg within hours rather than months or years. The Hasan Daegian army never stood a chance against the lightning speed of the Bhuttanian army in the grips of the wizard's enchantment.

As soon as Dorak took control of the capital O Konya, the spell disbursed, and now everyone moved normally. Mikkotto twisted her lips in annoyance. Too bad. She wished the spell had lasted until she could discover the whereabouts of her royal cousin.

Mikkotto jerked her head up. She faintly heard Dorak ordering, "BHUTTANIANS! ALL WEAPONS ON THE FLOOR!"

She cursed knowing Dorak had found Abisola and her consort. Fortunately for her, she had placed men among various squads, giving them instructions to kill the queen and her husband if they came upon them.

Grinning, she relished the thought that they would

obey her and not Dorak, paying them with gold and the promise of more coins and land to come if they carried out her orders. Greed was a great motivator to get the unpleasantries of life done by those who valued money above all else.

Still, Mikkotto couldn't take a chance. She scampered up the grand white marble staircase, jumping over slain bodies until she reached the second floor. Hearing screaming, she ran up another flight with her women warriors following behind.

Motioning for her warriors to wait, Mikkotto peered into a doorway and saw Dorak and a few Bhuttanians threatening Abisola and Iasos, who huddled on the floor before a small staircase going to the rooftop. Between them stood Maura, brandishing a sword. Behind her stood two Dinii with their talons exposed, looking very threatening.

The Dinii gave Mikkotto pause. She did not care to have her face slashed again nor die from a quick cut across her throat with their razor sharp nails. If truth be known, Mikkotto was terrified of them, but that fear had to be put aside. Victory was given to the bold, not the fearful.

Mikkotto studied the Dinii, thinking the taller one was Empress Gitar. She had seen her briefly at Maura's birthday celebration before her son bumbled Maura's assassination. Although the attempt on Maura's life had failed, Mikkotto had not flinched when told of her son's death at the hand of a Dini. She had little faith in her only son's ability and was only too glad she had not assigned one of her daughters to the task. Daughters were precious, but sons were expendable.

She motioned to her warriors to be quiet while she listened to the conversation between Dorak and Abisola. If Maura and her parents were killed, Dorak would make her queen of Hasan Daeg. If he decided to spare them, she would have to make a daring move and quickly too.

Moving closer, Mikkotto heard Dorak speak, "Princess Maura, we meet again." Dorak looked around the great hallway. "I see that you and your party have dispatched a few more of my men. I'm afraid I will have to put a stop to that."

Kill her. KILL HER! thought Mikkotto, hugging the darkness of the doorway.

Concentrating on Dorak, Maura did not see Mikkotto slinking closer and closer.

Dorak stepped nearer to Queen Abisola, now being held upright in the arms of Iasos.

Maura and Yeti immediately blocked his way.

Dorak held up his hands in supplication. "Princess, I only want to speak to your mother," he said calmly.

Looking past Maura, he uttered, "Queen Abisola, it is over. The city has been taken and is in my control."

Queen Abisola groaned.

Dorak continued in a soothing voice. "Your Majesty, I will give you the best terms for surrender. You and your family will not be harmed. Look, as you can see, my men have put down their arms. It is not my desire to destroy this wondrous city. Your family may still sit on the throne as long as you pay homage to me as liege lord. My people need food. We need it desperately. Give me what I want, and I will make Hasan Daeg a power to behold within the Bhuttanian Empire." Dorak took another step toward Queen Abisola.

NO! NO! What is Dorak doing? I was promised Hasan Daeg by his father. Dorak can't do this to me, Mikkotto screamed in her head. She had to make her move soon.

Maura brought up her sword.

Dorak walked up to the blade pointed at his throat. He stood so that the point of the weapon almost pierced his skin. "Princess, I beseech you. Nothing can be gained from this last stand. It is over."

"I can kill you right now."

"Then you would sign your death warrant. My men would kill you and your parents before you made it to the roof," Dorak replied softly. "You would be of no use to your people then, I assure you."

"But neither would you."

Dorak chuckled softly. "You are a most unusual young woman. I do hope I will be present to witness your final blooming, but that is up to you."

When Maura did not respond to his words, Dorak turned his attention to the failing Hasan Daegian queen. "Queen Abisola, think about your daughter. Surely you do not want to see her die. Surrender. It is all you can do."

The queen struggled. She coughed, and blood seeped from her mouth.

Iasos quickly wiped it with his sleeve.

Holding tightly to her husband's arms, Abisola whispered, "You may take me. But all of the Dinii, including Empress Gitar and my child, are to leave now." She looked at Iasos. "My husband will share my fate with me."

"Mother, no!" Maura insisted.

"This is my final command. Start withdrawing. Now!" Abisola croaked.

"I am afraid I cannot allow this," interjected Dorak.

Queen Abisola measured her words carefully. "Aga Dorak, I am over three hundred years old. Only recently have I begun to age. Even your magicians have no spells to do this. Do you not want to know my secret? Do you not want to live for a long time? How long did your

father live? He wasn't even fifty and was used up."
Abisola took a deep breath, which made a wheezing
noise. "Just think of what you could accomplish in three
hundred years or maybe more. Let my daughter go with
the Dinii, and once they are safely away, I will show you
how it is done." She let her words sink in.

Mikkotto knew it was now or never. "She's lying.
The Bogazkoy will never accept a male bonding!" she
cried from the shadows.

"Mikkotto!" exclaimed Iasos. "You traitorous mon-
grel!"

Dorak swung around, and upon seeing Mikkotto, his
eyes narrowed. "How did you get up here?"

Mikkotto laughed. "The front door was wide open.
There was no one to stop me. It seems everyone below
is dead." She moved closer.

"Stop where you are," commanded Maura, her skin
prickling from the tension.

"Is that any way to talk to your cousin?" Mikkotto
cooed.

Dorak shot Mikkotto a surprised look.

Mikkotto grinned. "That is right, my dear Dorak. I
used to play in these very hallways as a child. My mother
was Abisola's first cousin and Lady Sari's daughter. For
you see, Lady Sari is Marchioness Sari Sumsumitoyo and
third in line to the throne. She gave up her title to serve

the House of de Magela, stupid woman that she is." She moved forward.

Dorak blocked her way. "I swear to you, Mikkotto, if you do not leave, I am going to kill you with my own hands."

"I think you have forgotten that we have a deal. I am to rule Hasan Daeg in exchange for certain services rendered."

"You, queen?" Iasos snorted in disgust.

"I made no deal with you to be queen," denied Dorak. "I merely said I would let you live if you showed me the location of O Konya. I am sorry to say I regret that decision. I now have new plans for you." Dorak, wearing an expression of hate, moved toward Mikkotto with deadly purpose.

Realizing Dorak's intention, Mikkotto shoved Dorak into Maura. "NOW!" she shrieked.

Several soldiers pulled daggers from their sleeves and threw them at the royal couple.

One struck Abisola in the heart, killing her instantly.

The other hit Iasos in the stomach. He crumpled with his hands around the dagger, trying to pull it out.

Maura screamed, scrambling over the bloody floor and throwing herself across her parents.

Chaun Maaun, having recovered from the arduous journey, rushed down the steps. He pushed his mother and Yeti behind him. Seeing Maura curled over the body of her mother and her dying father, he let out a muffled cry.

Dorak stood between the Hasan Daegians and his soldiers with his arms outstretched.

Other Bhuttanian warriors rushed forward to restrain the men who had thrown the daggers.

Mikkotto scurried away with her guards running interference before her. They collided with a squad of Bhuttanians loyal to Dorak. Thinking quickly, Mikkotto pointed and barked, "Hurry, your master is in danger. The Dinii empress is upstairs and threatening Dorak. Save him!"

She and her women pressed against the wall, letting the heavily-armed men rush past her to the third floor as they all heard Dorak shouting commands and trying to gain control of the grave situation.

Not wanting to linger where Dorak could seize her, Mikkotto pulled free a lance sticking out from the gut of a Hasan Daegian warrior and knocked a Bhuttanian soldier off his warhorse with it.

Jumping upon the giant creature, Mikkotto gave orders, "Get yourselves horses and catch up with me at my estate. We will regroup and hide in Camaroon. There must be another way to the throne of Hasan Daeg, and I swear to you, my good women, I will find it!"

Mikkotto kicked the anxious horse and rode off.

When Dorak rushed out of the palace with his men, not a trace of Mikkotto could be found even with a massive hunt looking for her.

It was as though Kaseri had swallowed her up.

Mikkotto was gone!

1

orak carried Maura to her chamber.

He laid Maura carefully on her bed and summoned a
healer. As he waited, Dorak smoothed Maura's furrowed brow and held her hand. Gently, he kissed the
tips of her fingers.

A guard soon appeared with Meagan of Skujpor.
Her traditional white robe was soaked red with blood.
Seeing the patient was the princess, Meagan rushed to
the bedside and pushed Dorak out of the way. She
examined Maura with great care. Finally, she sighed with
relief.

"What is wrong with her?" asked Dorak, offended
by the healer's brusque treatment.

"She's in shock," replied Meagan, pushing red hair
out of her face. She pointed to the princess' skin. "This
blood is not hers."

"How do you know?"

"Because it is red. Her blood is blue." She paused for a moment. "It must be her father's."

"When will she recover?"

The healer looked at Dorak with distaste. "When her mind can absorb the shock of this terrible day. Until then, she will stay as she is." Meagan stood directly in front of Dorak, confronting him. "I will come back to check on the princess, but now I must go back to the wounded. They need me more."

Dorak did not stop her as she moved toward the door. "I will send an escort with you and have my physician accompany you."

"That is not necessary. I have seen your healers in action and do not approve of their methods." Meagan turned as if an afterthought. "If you wish for us to treat your men, send them over. They will have a greater chance of survival with our medicine."

"You would help your enemy?" asked Dorak, confused.

"It is you whom I wish to kill," Meagan replied simply. There was a moment of unnatural silence between Dorak and the woman he knew could help Maura. "I will help any injured animal, including your men," said Meagan, breaking the angry quiet. Then she was gone.

Dorak, relieved that Maura had no serious physical injuries, went out into the hallway and found his second-in-command.

The commander, yelling orders at his men, immediately came to attention and pressed his fist to his chest.

"Are there any survivors from the court or noble houses?" asked Dorak.

"Yes, Great Aga. They are guarded in the royal stables."

Dorak raised an eyebrow.

The commander looked sheepishly at him. "Great Aga, this palace does not have a dungeon. I had nowhere else to put them."

"Get some of the noblewomen and have them stay with the princess—I mean, the queen—in her chambers. Then take the bodies of Queen Abisola and Consort Iasos to the throne room. Have women attend them." Dorak fell silent.

The commander waited a long time before Dorak spoke again.

"There is to be no looting. Tell the men that no citizens are to be harmed upon pain of death. Is that understood?"

"Yes, Great Aga. Your word is law." The commander waited to be excused.

"Send the Black Cacodemon to me. You will no

doubt find him lurking around the dying."

The commander's eyes widened. "Yes, Great Aga," he replied in a weak voice.

Dorak strode away, leaving the commander to search for someone else to carry his message to the Black Cacodemon. He would rather face ten hostile Dinii than speak one word to that foul wizard who stood among the dying inhaling their souls as they departed their bodies.

Finally, he spied a young lieutenant and called him over. With a faint smile, the commander gave the young man his instructions and watched the color drain from the boy's face. With a strong push to his back, the commander sent the lieutenant off and proceeded to the stables.

Dorak returned to Maura's bedchamber. From the balcony of her room, he watched his men putting out fires in the city and restoring order. The dead were being collected and laid into long lines. Tomorrow, he would let the Hasan Daegians mourn their departed loved ones and put them to rest according to their customs. He would honor his own fallen with purifying fires in accordance with the Bhuttanian way. Then he would start building his empire. He looked at Maura. "The dead did not sacrifice in vain. Together, you and I will build a new order."

He leaned on the balcony railing, surveying the city. "The greatest the world has ever seen."

Maura did not hear Dorak. Dreaming, she heard only her screams as a dagger pierced her mother's heart. Again and again, the scene replayed itself until her mother, dead on the floor, opened her lifeless eyes and said, "Leave this place of death and rejoin the living. I will always be with you."

A shimmering woman appeared. She floated toward Maura and held her hands against Maura's temples. "Sleep. Sleep. Find comfort in the darkness. Morning will come soon enough." The horrible images slowly faded from Maura's mind as she drifted into a deep slumber.

2

Maura opened her eyes.

The first thing she saw was the royal physician in spotless white robes, bending over her bed with a puzzled look in her eyes.

"You look tired, Meagan," spoke Maura, noting the dark circles under Meagan's eyes.

Ignoring the remark, Meagan asked, "How do you feel, Your Majesty?"

Maura winced at the word *Majesty* and was overwhelmed with a flood of painful memories. "My mother?" she asked weakly.

The healer wiped a tear from her cheek and shook her white-capped head with wisps of red hair peeking out.

"Father too?"

"He died shortly after the queen passed away. I must

add that he died without much pain. He wrote a letter for you, but I do not know what happened to it." The healer sat on the bed and patted Maura's shoulder. "I want you to know that they were treated with respect and honor as befitting your mother's glorious reign."

Maura sat up, alarmed. "How long have I been unconscious?"

"Nine days," boomed a masculine voice from the balcony.

Maura looked past Meagan, squinting her eyes and holding her hand up against the strong rays of the sun bouncing off the white balcony.

Silhouetted against the white-hot light, a dark figure emerged from the filmy curtains separating the room from the balcony. Dorak strode lazily over to the bed.

The healer bowed and left the room.

Dorak towered over Maura. He had a worried look on his face. He was unshaven, and his hair had not seen a comb for some time. Dressed in a black shirt with black breeches tucked into worn black boots, Maura thought he looked like a convict or, even worse, a privateer. His dark brooding look frightened her.

"I was very worried about you, Queen Maura," said Dorak, pouring her a glass of water. "I was beginning to wonder if you were ever going to open your eyes again."

Maura drank greedily. Her mouth felt hot and dirty.

The cool water soothed her raw throat. "I wish I had never awakened," she spat.

Dorak gave her an appraising look. "You look awful."

"So do you," Maura replied, returning the stare.

"Never at a loss for words, are you?"

"Why are you here with me? Isn't there someone who needs butchering somewhere?"

"Your . . . *our* country is in safe hands. Its citizens are safe. Law and order have been restored. The fires have been put out."

"You mean after you murdered the lawful queen and invaded a peaceful nation to which you have no legitimate claim?"

Dorak grew angry. "I had nothing to do with the death of your parents. I swear to you before Bhuttu!"

Feeling her eyes tearing, Maura struggled to retain her composure. "You will never know how much I hate you! I will not rest until you and your cohorts are thrown out of Hasan Daeg!"

A wicked smile grew on Dorak's handsome face. "That will pose something of a problem since I intend to marry you."

Maura gasped and drew back.

Dorak's smile grew broader as he saw her panic. "I am going to leave now." He put out his hands as if to stop her from pleading. "No, my indigo queen, don't try to stop me. Matters of state. I am sure you understand."

Sneering, Maura turned her face away. "I'll die first before I marry you. You know I can make it happen."

Dorak pinched her cheek and laughed. He strode out of the room as if in good humor. Once out of sight, Dorak's expression grew serious. He motioned to the healer Meagan, who waited in the hallway with several noblewomen. Meagan's white robes fluttered in the breeze of the marble hallway as she went over to him. She bowed and waited for Dorak to speak.

He seemed confused and rubbed his temples as if in pain.

"Do you have a headache, my lord?" she asked.

Dorak ignored her question. "The queen is depressed. She threatened to take her life."

"That is understandable considering the circumstances."

"I have heard stories that Hasan Daegian rulers can will themselves to die."

"Anyone can will themselves to death if unhappy enough."

"I want the queen watched. Make sure she eats. Stop her if she tries to do anything foolish."

The healer raised an eyebrow. "Sire, you can rest assured that I will do everything in my power to ensure the queen's health returns. However, I will never help you enslave her."

"You people constantly surprise me. I would have anyone from my country executed who talked to me the way you just did. Since you are not Bhuttanian I give you allowance, but that will not last forever."

"Of course, my lord, but you came seeking us and not the other way around." Meagan bowed and briskly walked away, calling to her assistants who were struggling to carry her medical bags. She knocked on the queen's door before entering.

Behind her followed several noblewomen who had consecrated their lives to become healers. Gone were the necklaces made of precious stones. Gone were the flowers woven into the hair. Gone were the costly robes of rare cloth. Now they wore the stern black robes of the initiate, allowing only their family crest embroidered on their chest for adornment.

Hearing no reply, Meagan opened the door and peered into the room.

The queen lay on the bed in a fetal position with her eyes tightly shut. Maura did not stir.

Meagan checked Maura's eyes. Startled by what she saw, she called discreetly for Lady Sari so word would not pass to Dorak that something was wrong.

Lady Sari came as swiftly as her old bones would

carry her. She hovered over Maura, wringing her hands.

"What is the meaning of this?" asked Meagan, pulling open Maura's eyes. The eyes had become a solid blue, blocking out any sign of a pupil or iris. The effect was chilling to one who had never seen it before.

Sari gasped at the sight.

"I have read ancient treatises that discuss the care and nurturing of the Royal House of Hasan Daeg. There is no mention that the queens' eyes ever turned a solid blue for any reason," Meagan stated.

"That is because we are not allowed to touch the body until it is over. By then, the eyes return to normal."

"Body? You talk as though this girl is dead."

Sari's face assumed a look of intense sorrow. "For all intents, she is. She has taken herself into the *death dream*. There is nothing more you can do."

"Hasan Daegian queens will only do that if they are over three hundred years old and have produced a suitable heir. She is neither old nor has she had a child."

Sari looked softly at Meagan. "You did not read enough. Hasan Daegian queens can will themselves to die if they are in terrible pain." She straightened Maura's coverlet. "And this child is in terrible pain. She does not have the will to go on."

Meagan blustered.

"You do not understand. They reach a certain nadir and this just happens. It is nothing they can control. Dorak must have said something to cause this."

"In most ancient writings, there is mentioned a tree as a giver of life to the Royal House alone. It is written that there is some sort of blending between the ruler and the tree." The healer took Sari's hand in her calloused ones. "You have been with this family all of your life. Do you know of such a tree? I have done all I can. I fear that if I do not bring her out of this self-induced coma, she will die this time."

Saying nothing, Sari went deep into thought.

Meagan was quiet. She was a healer, but she had been exposed to politics long enough to understand the significance of Sari's silence. "Do you know of a tree that can save this queen? Help me for I can do no more!"

The old woman shook her head slowly and clasped her hands in despair. She had the air of defeat about her. "There is such a plant, but it cannot help her. It is also dying."

"How does it work? I must try something." Meagan felt Maura's pulse. "If her heart gets any slower, we are going to lose her!"

"I will take you to it, but we must bring the queen."

"How can we remove her from this room without

suspicion?"

Sari gave a weak smile. "Not all of our teeth are gone. We can bite a little yet. Follow me."

Confused, Meagan ordered her assistants to carry the limp queen.

Sari went to a wall and pressed a certain stone.

Silently, part of the wall opened into a small, narrow hallway.

3

Sari entered.

She poked her head back out of the passageway and motioned for the healer to follow her.

Meagan grabbed an oil lamp, lit it, and taking a deep breath, entered.

The black-robed women followed, carrying the moaning queen. One of the noblewomen placed her hand over the queen's mouth. The door closed, leaving the group feeling isolated and confined.

"Watch where you are going," Sari cautioned. "We will soon begin descending. The steps are sometimes slippery."

The group silently followed the old woman down the stone steps, their footfalls echoing loudly against the massive hand-hewn walls. Down and down they went, descending far below the city. They could hear the noisy hubbub of the market, and the traffic on the main boulevard of O Konya.

With Sari leading the way, Meagan held the lamp high above her head, so the light spread unevenly but brightly on the walkway. She was surprised that the ancient passageway was clean of debris. Her breathing was not impeded by mold or dust. She wondered who kept the underground passages clean.

Coming to the bottom of the stairs, the initiates placed Maura gently on the stone floor and rested, panting deeply. Some wiped the sweat off their foreheads and the back of their necks with the hems of their robes.

Sari motioned them forward.

Without complaining, they picked up their royal cargo and resumed following the older woman deeper into the passageway. There were many corridors, but Sari consistently traveled down the farthest left.

Meagan took careful note of this, as well as the presence of a gentle breeze in the corridor, a fact she tucked away.

Sari took another left and came upon double wooden doors with carvings of ancient, mystical, and religious symbols. Although they were not locked, Sari did not have the strength to open the massive doors by herself.

Meagan and several of the initiates pulled at the iron

handles, which formed the image of pouncing uultepes.

Groaning, the doors opened an inch at a time.

One of the smaller women wiggled through a crack between the doors and then pushed from the opposite side as the doors opened out into the corridor. Frightened, she dared not look behind as strange sounds reverberated in the darkness. She was glad when the heavy doors opened wide, and lamplight spilled beyond her.

Sari and the Anqarian healer stepped beyond the doors into a voluminous chamber.

The older woman watched Meagan's face as she discovered the secret of the de Magela family. "Behold, the Tree of Life!" Sari whispered.

Meagan took everything in.

The cavernous chamber contained a small lake. Steam hissed from the water's surface, and Meagan could make out a small island of green rock at its center. In the middle of the island stood a blue plant with wide, flat tendrils extending beyond the rock and into the steaming water.

"There is a boat over there," Sari pointed. "You and I alone must take the queen. The boat will not hold all of us."

"That's the Bogazkoy?" asked Meagan, looking at the limp, unimpressive plant.

Sari barked a cruel laugh. "That's the Tree of Life or rather what is left of it. It may be too weak to do the queen any good now. It has not been used for almost ten years."

"That is when Queen Abisola started to age," commented Meagan.

Sari nodded. "Queen Abisola wanted what was left of its power for her daughter." Sari instructed the initiates to follow her and place the queen into a small rowboat.

Meagan looked skeptically at the rickety boat but tucked the hem of her robes in her belt determinedly. "Why is the boat in such poor condition?"

"As I told you. Queen Abisola did not want to use what was left of the Bogazkoy's power, so we rarely came down here. The hot water must have rotted the wood."

Meagan climbed precariously into the boat as it rocked back and forth. She tried to steady herself by grabbing the oars.

Sari climbed in after her and immediately sat down. She checked Maura's breathing. It seemed labored. Taking the wooden oars from Meagan, Sari began rowing toward the green island.

Meagan placed her hand in the steaming water, pulling it back quickly. "It's almost scalding!"

Sari nodded. "The lake is fed by a hot mineral spring. The Bogazkoy needs the minerals to survive. Taste it."

Meagan gingerly placed her fingertip in the water and then to her tongue. "It's salty, but we are hundreds of miles from the sea."

Sari looked at her with a knowing smile. "Yes."

Meagan thought she saw something move under the water and peered closer to get a better look.

"If I were you, I would not put my nose too close to the water," Sari cautioned.

"Is something down there?" asked Meagan, pointing to the black, bubbling water.

"I have never seen anything, but things do not feel right to me. Maybe it is because my nerves are so fraught. Princess Maura has never been here before—I mean the queen." Sari looked uneasily around the chamber.

Meagan shuddered and put her hands in her lap. "Do you think we are safe in this thing?"

Sari dipped the oars silently into the lake. "I don't know. I have never done this before."

"What?"

"I always stood back where your women are. I have never been across the water. I cannot swim."

Meagan blinked several times. She felt her left eyebrow twitch.

Sari grew silent and said no more, concentrating on rowing until the boat reached the rock island, scraping against it.

Meagan pulled the boat closer to the island dock and climbed out.

Sari handed her a battered rope with which to tie the boat.

Meagan stood on the wooden dock, noticing that many of its planks looked rotten. She whispered a prayer that the boards would hold. Leaning over, she helped Sari pull Maura from the boat.

Sari, not used to such a heavy load, almost dropped the young woman into the bubbling water.

Meagan heard her women cry out.

"Oh dear," was all Sari could muster, upset at her lapse, but became horrified when something went under the boat and raised it out of the water several inches.

With a heavy fog blowing in her face, it was hard for Meagan to see what circled the rowboat, but she knew it was large. Reaching down, she pulled with all her might and dragged Maura from the boat. She felt the wooden planks start to give under her. With a mighty lunge, Meagan jumped onto a small outcropping of rocks with Maura on her shoulders.

Maura slid off and landed with a hard thud.

Meagan then extended a hand to Sari. As Sari reached for the healer's plump but sturdy hand, the boat rocked a second time, and she lost her balance again.

Meagan saw a green motley creature swim away and turn, making its way to the boat again. "Lady Sari, hurry!"

The older woman looked over her shoulder and saw the monster swimming toward her. Her eyes wide with fright, Sari scrambled to the edge of the rowboat and jumped as the boat was smashed into pieces. A great wave of hot spray hit her.

Tearing at Sari's hair and clothes, Meagan pulled her up.

They both clung to the dripping rocks, catching their breath.

Sari's hands and face were bleeding where they had scraped against the jagged stones.

Meagan held a hunk of Sari's white hair in her hand. "Here, I think this is yours," she said, trying to put the hair back on Sari's head.

Both women broke into laughter.

Meagan's attention was diverted when she spied the Bogazkoy extending its blue tendrils slowly over Maura's body. She suppressed a shudder. "It's alive," she mumbled.

"It knows the queen is here," said Sari, her breathing

relaxing.

"What do we do?"

"Let us pull her closer to the plant. Queen Abisola used to stand in the center of the island, and it would wrap itself around her."

Grasping the queen under the arms, Meagan dragged Maura toward the plant. If she stepped on tendrils, they would writhe upward as if in agony.

Sari followed, helping as best she could.

"Here! Here is the center of the tree," said Sari. They gently placed Maura at the foot of the main trunk.

Meagan folded the queen's hands.

"Step back," Sari ordered.

Meagan jumped over the moving tendrils and stood by Sari, reaching for her hand. They waited together, clasping their hands tightly.

Slowly, all of the Bogazkoy's tendrils retracted from the water and moved over the rocks, searching for the queen. Upon finding her, they wrapped themselves around the unconscious girl until Maura was not visible.

Alarmed, Meagan started forward.

Sari caught her arm and held her back. "This is what the Bogazkoy does."

"She won't be able to breathe," Meagan argued.

"Yes, she will. Let the Bogazkoy do its magic if it has any power left." Sari shrugged. "And if it cannot, what difference will it make for the queen to die anyway?"

Finding no fault in Sari's logic, Meagan sat on her haunches studying the Tree Of Life.

The tendrils wrapped themselves around Maura so tightly as to become a second skin. An acrid smell filled the air. Maura began to twitch inside her cocoon.

Meagan glanced nervously at Sari.

Sari smiled. "It is injecting its serum into our lady. It has some life in it yet."

"What kind of serum?"

"I do not know, but when the queen arises, she will have little puncture wounds over her body, and her orifices will be sore."

"All of them?"

"Yes," replied Sari, looking off into the rolling water. "That is why it is referred to as a 'mating.'"

"Oh," was all Meagan could comment.

The cocoon continued to jerk and twitch, seeming impervious to anything surrounding it.

Meagan soon gained the courage to touch the tendrils. They did not respond to her. Inside the cocoon, she could hear gurgling noises.

"Do not worry," Sari comforted. "This is normal."

"Did Queen Abisola ever complain about pain during this procedure?"

Sari grinned. "The only thing she ever said to me was that it was like being loved by six different men at the same time."

"Well, that could hurt," replied Meagan, feeling the conversation was taking on a disrespectful tone.

"Or it could be ecstasy. It depends on one's frame of reference."

It was Meagan's turn to snort. She continued watching, taking mental notes until she glanced forlornly at the broken pieces of the dock and the rowboat floating in the water. She would think about getting across the water later. Right now, she had a queen to save.

The initiates waited patiently on the other side, occasionally waving and calling. Some prayed to Mekonia, their nature goddess.

A loud wail came from the cocoon. The cry wavered and then fell silent.

Sari rushed to the blue-wrapped mass. "Help me!" she cried. "This is not right!"

Meagan helped Sari tear the tendrils from Maura.

They had become brittle and broke off, crumbling into dust. After removing many layers of plant wrap, they could see their queen. Her clothes were shredded.

Hastily, the healer pulled plant material from Maura's nose and ears. Realizing the tendrils had crumbled inside her mouth, she reached inside and scooped out the debris. She rolled the young queen over, trying to get her to expel plant material on her own. She hit Maura between the shoulder blades. Getting no response, she pummeled again and again.

4

aura coughed.

She spat debris onto the rocks.

"Good," Sari encouraged. "Get it all out."

Exhausted, Maura stretched out, breathing heavily. There was a pile of dead Bogazkoy tendrils beside her. She opened her eyes and stared at Sari who peered down anxiously, and then at Meagan who was taking her pulse.

The queen's skin was a much darker hue and swollen with tiny punctures. There was another change in Maura that Meagan had a hard time deciphering, but the queen seemed to radiate life. An aura of soothing heat surrounded her. Meagan had the sudden urge to dry her wet clothes on Maura's skin.

"The Royal Bogazkoy is dead," Maura muttered. "It gave me all it had left." She began pulling dead tendrils from her hair. Laughing bitterly, she said, "Sari, you must not approve of how I look. I certainly don't look like royalty. How the nobles would fret over my lack of decorum."

Meagan and Sari laughed as well, both aware of the irony of the situation.

"Well, frankly, I have seen you look better," replied Sari, her eyes full of relief.

"I have news for you, Sari. Most of your hair is gone."

"Thanks to this heavy-handed know-it-all."

"That's the thanks I get for saving you from the creature," growled Meagan.

"What creature?" Maura asked.

Sari pointed to the water. "That thing there."

Maura peered over into the water and caught a glimpse of something skimming the surface. She was astonished. "My mother never mentioned anything about a creature in the water."

"I have never seen it before," Sari said.

Maura thought for a moment. "This must be some evil work of the Black Cacodemon trying to prevent me from getting to the Royal Bogazkoy." She looked appraisingly at Meagan and Sari. "Good work, women. I salute you."

"Why do you say that, Your Majesty?" Meagan

asked.

"I did not put myself in the death dream of my own will. Something has been compelling me to do so."

Sari put her hand up to her mouth. "The Black Cacodemon again!"

"Sari, do you think I am so cowardly that I would leave my people at their hour of greatest need?"

"So much has happened. I have not had time to think."

Maura nodded her head. "How well I am beginning to know that feeling." She looked around and acknowledged the greetings from the initiates standing on the other side of the lake. "The question now is how do we get from here to over there?" She pointed to the initiates and carefully perused what was left of the dock and the boat. Then she spied the doors. "I wonder if those doors float? You, over there!" Maura shouted. "Get one of those doors and put it in the water."

The noblewomen looked at each other and then back to the little group on the island.

Maura motioned toward the giant doors. "Get a door off its hinges, and paddle it over here."

Sari argued, "Oh, Your Majesty, that is too dangerous."

"Do you want to swim? This is our only option at the moment, or we could send the women back for

Dorak. I am sure he would love to know about the Bogazkoy and how the Hasan Daegian queens are so long-lived."

Sari bowed her head in acquiescence.

One of the noblewomen found a large rock and began beating at the lower iron hinge. The rock broke against it.

Another initiate found a larger rock, taking two women to raise it and strike against the rusty hinge. It took a great deal of sweat and effort, but the initiates finally removed the bolt out of the hinge. The door made a grinding sound as it shifted its weight.

The noblewomen then climbed atop one another forming a pyramid. The top two women lifted the rock over their grunting comrades. They dropped the rock once and had to climb down to retrieve it. This process went on for what seemed hours, but finally, they managed to knock the last bolt out.

The door teetered toward the pyramid. One of the women lunged forward and pushed the door away from them. The sudden motion caused the precariously balanced women to tumble to the ground. At the same time, the carved door landed with a thunderous crash.

One by one, the women sat up, rubbing their heads and arms. They checked each other for broken bones, and when satisfied, they waved back. Only one woman was slightly injured, and the others improvised a sling for her arm.

Maura sighed with relief. "Thrust the door into the water. See if it floats," she called over.

The noblewomen laboriously dragged the door to the water. One woman ripped her skirt into strips and made a rope, which she tied on the door handle.

With a great push, the door was shoved into the water.

Meagan held her breath, and closing her eyes, she clutched Sari's hands, asking, "Is it floating? Oh, by the good Goddess, let it float!" She peeked with one eye and then immediately closed it again. "I cannot stand this excitement."

Sari retorted, "Quit your whining. Try this adventure at my age."

Maura leapt triumphantly in the air. "It works. It's not sinking!"

Remembering she was now queen, she composed herself. "Two of you women climb aboard and paddle over here," she commanded.

Two of the younger women sat on the rock's shoulder and jumped on the wooden door now serving as a raft.

The door rocked, and for a moment, Maura thought it would capsize.

The black-robed assistants quickly spread themselves out on the raft and steadied it so that it rocked gently on the boiling current. Once steady, they sat up and tore their skirts. Wrapping long pieces of cloth around one of their hands and arms to protect their skin from the hot water, they lay on the edges of the door and began paddling.

The women, remaining on the shore, yelled encouragement. One initiate, with a particularly loud voice, counted the stroke beats for them. Everyone else became quiet as the woman counted.

They were halfway across when Sari yelled, "LOOK OUT!"

A creature, with shiny green scales and barbed protruding teeth, rose out of the water, attacking the raft. It picked up one screaming woman and pulled her down into the murky depths.

Bubbles rose to the surface and diminished until there were none.

Then only stillness.

No one made a sound. Only the rolling of the water could be heard. The woman still alive on the raft was dazed and confused.

Suddenly, Maura pierced the stunned silence. "STROKE! Keep on. I am giving you an order, you worthless piece of flotsam. Stroke! Stroke! Stroke!"

The woman, responding to the firm voice, got over her shock and took up the count again. When she came to a piece of wood from the disintegrated rowboat, she used it as a paddle.

Nervously, Maura peered into the water. She could see no sign of the beast.

Sweating profusely, the initiate made it to the rock island without further incident. She threw the skirt-twisted rope to Maura who tied it around a large boulder.

The queen helped her climb up.

The initiate tried to bow.

Maura waved her away. "Go rest. Save your strength for the journey back."

The woman did as told, collapsing on the rocks.

Meagan checked the woman's burns from the hot water.

"You think we can get across with that creature?" Meagan asked, unwrapping the steaming bandages from the woman's arms. "It will be suicide."

Maura looked over her shoulder at the water. "She made it."

"With one dead."

"That is right," Maura replied. "Only one is dead."

"This is appalling," Meagan said, not quite believing their situation.

"Yes, you speak the truth. It is appalling that Anqara was burned to the ground. It is appalling that my parents are dead. It is appalling that my country has been invaded, and my crown taken. The list goes on and on. I can sit on this stupid rock and cry myself into oblivion, or I can go back and try to save something." Maura's eyes narrowed. "Healer, what do you suggest I do?"

Ashamed, Meagan bowed. She knew that she lacked Maura's resolve.

"Your Majesty, can you send for help?" Sari asked, thinking of the Dinii.

"I have no magic powers, Sari. The Dinii taught me to fight well, but I never could master telepathy long range."

"But I heard that Hasan Daegian queens can heal," Meagan ventured.

Maura regarded the worn-out initiate nursing her burns. "I dare not try it. I need all my strength to get back across." She sat down, her courage deserting her momentarily.

"But you are a good warrior."

Maura brightened. "Yes, Sari, I am a good warrior."

"Then get up, little sparrow, and fight. The day is not over, and I do not want to die on this barren rock pile." She smiled tenderly at Maura and held out her hand.

Maura pulled herself up and touched Sari's cheek. "If I must die, good Sari, it will be an honor to die at your side. But I do not think that will be today." She turned to Meagan. "As soon as your woman is able, we will gather what wood we can from the dock and boat."

"For what purpose, Your Majesty?"

"To make spears, of course. And we will need good rocks to grind the wood into points. Get busy. We have much to do."

Meagan walked away. "Why of course. We will just make spears," she muttered to herself in a mocking tone. "Why didn't I think of that?"

"I hope Dorak doesn't wander into your chamber to check on you," Sari mused, suddenly worried. "I do not think we could explain your absence."

"Let us hope matters of state keep him away for a long time," Maura said. The mention of Dorak brought back painful memories. For the first time, she thought of Chaun Maaun. She wondered if he was safe in the City of the Peaks. Realizing she missed him terribly, she pushed the thought from her mind and concentrated on the crisis at hand.

I can do this! she thought. Relaxing somewhat, she searched for a grinding stone. Daydreams and longing for Chaun Maaun would have to wait.

After several hours, the women had gathered many planks of wood.

Maura sharpened them into points, although she was sorry there was no fire to harden them, she would have to work with what she had.

Finally, they were ready!

The initiate bound her arms with rags again as did Meagan.

Maura and Sari sat in the middle.

Cautiously, they climbed onto the bobbing raft. For several hours, they had seen no sign of the creature and were not anxious to announce they were leaving the island.

The women quietly dipped their rough-looking oars into the rolling water and began paddling back to the other shore.

The initiates waited for them with hands folded inside their long black sleeves. Their faces were devoid of expression as they watched the raft make its way toward them. Suddenly, one of them cried out, "It comes! It comes!"

Maura jerked her head around and caught sight of something sliding under the raft. A large fantail sprayed hot water on them. "It's going under! Hold on!"

Picking up a spear, she leaned on the side where the creature emerged and jabbed hard into the water, striking deep into its flesh. The spear broke, leaving Maura with only a short jagged stick.

The beast submerged in the dark water.

Maura leaned from side to side looking for the creature.

"Paddle! Paddle!" Sari encouraged, her face white with fear.

Without warning, the serpent-like monster rose from the water with a deafening roar.

Sari clamped her hands tightly over her ears.

Gusts of scalding water sprayed the women as they clutched the raft now swirling around and around uncontrollably.

A long, black barbed tongue violently lashed out and struck Meagan in the face. Stunned, Meagan did not resist as the slimy band wrapped her head and tried to pull her into the water.

Seeing Meagan helpless, Maura repeatedly stabbed at the monstrous tongue until her spear sliced through the tough tissue. The creature released Meagan and began to submerge.

"Hang onto the tongue!" Maura shouted. She dropped her spear and grabbed the injured tongue oozing foul smelling blood. "Help me! I need to keep its head above water!"

Numb with fear, Meagan grabbed the odious band

of tissue.

Sari got behind Meagan and helped to anchor her.

Now bucking with its fantail, the beast tried to flip the raft into the swirling water.

Maura frantically looked for her spear, but it had fallen into the water like the others.

The initiate threw to Maura the last surviving weapon.

Maura took careful aim and shoved the spear into the creature's left eye.

It writhed in pain. Hanging on, Maura thrust the spear in deeper until it reached its brain.

Giving one last cry, the sea serpent slowly sank into the murky depths of the lake.

Maura fell gasping on all fours. She looked at Meagan questioningly.

The healer nodded.

Maura took off what was left of her nightshirt, ripped it apart, and wrapped the rags around her hand. She lay down on her stomach and gave the order to paddle.

The initiate and Meagan put their arms into the hot water as well, as they had lost all of the makeshift oars. It took the battered survivors a long time to get to shore.

The waiting noblewomen greeted them somberly. One of the women tried to give Maura her robe.

Maura pushed the initiate's offer away. "Let me see your hands," she requested of Meagan, Sari, and the initiate. Maura placed their raw scorched flesh between hers and concentrated.

"Oh, my!" exclaimed Meagan. "It feels tingly." She looked at Maura with awe.

Sari mumbled a prayer and pulled her hand away, causing the bond to break with the other women. "That is enough, Maura. Do not waste your new strength on us."

Meagan studied her hands in astonishment. "I am almost healed. The blisters are gone. Just some redness and swelling left."

"Sari?" questioned Maura.

"I'm fine, little bird. Do not worry about me. I have more than enough energy to guide us home," Sari replied as she led them away from the lake.

Forming a single line, the women began the arduous journey back to the palace. No one said a word as they traveled through the corridors.

Reaching the stairs, they groaned with each step. Tired and hungry, they finally arrived at the top of the stairway.

Sari listened with her ear pressed next to the secret panel. Convinced no one was in the bedchamber, she cautiously opened the hidden door and entered Maura's room.

5

Sari opened the secret door.

The exhausted women crept into the bedroom.

"I hope you ladies had a good time on your journey," Dorak rasped as he lit a lamp in Maura's room.

Several of the women frantically turned around to seek shelter in the secret corridor, but the panel had already shut.

"And what is this? It is the good Queen Maura awake." He paused and took a hard look at the rags she was wearing. "I must say that is a fetching gown you have on there, Your Majesty. And what is that smell?" He sniffed the air. "It must be a new cologne, eau de sewer." He sat upright in his chair and crossed his arms. "You all smell that way. I guess that means you were together for a little escapade."

Maura, startled at the sight of Dorak, managed to

calm herself. "You are in my private quarters, my lord. I am asking you to leave."

Dorak ignored her. "You know, Your Majesty, my top general, Alexanee, has been turning this city upside down searching for you. I told him—NOOOO, she has not escaped. Queen Maura is just taking a little sightseeing tour of the city. She will be back. Well, he did not agree." Dorak stood and approached Maura, pushing several noblewomen out of the way. He caressed her shoulder with his index finger.

Maura held her breath and dared not look into his dark, menacing eyes.

Like a lover delivering words of endearment, Dorak whispered, "You will never guess how many people he has interrogated since your disappearance."

Maura flinched but remained silent.

"You are not playing the game, Your Majesty. Guess how many people have been rounded up and interrogated by my soldiers. Now, when I say interrogated, we Bhuttanians do more than ask questions." Dorak stopped his caressing and gloated. "Nod if you understand what I am implying."

Maura inclined her head.

"I think the last count of the interrogated who did not make it through the entire session was eight. If you do not believe me, take a look outside your window."

Maura staggered to a window and peered over the balcony railing. In the middle of the courtyard was a small stack of corpses. Maura resisted the urge to scream by crushing her lips tight.

Dorak came up behind her and whispered in her ear. "There was no need for this carnage. Let it be on your head."

She turned and faced him. "I was not trying to escape, I swear."

"I will make that determination after I have questioned these lovely ladies."

Maura grabbed his arm. "I'm asking you not to do this. I was not trying to escape."

"What were you doing?"

Maura looked away and said nothing.

"All right, ladies, you are to follow me. I have some nice gentlemen waiting for you," Dorak announced, pointing a short sword at them.

"Wait! Wait!" Maura pleaded. "If you hurt them, I shall will myself to die."

Dorak paused.

Maura realized how fearful he was of that happening. "You know I can do it, Dorak. I can will myself to die before sunrise, and there will be nothing your black wizard can do about it."

She came closer to him until she was almost touching his chest. "Dorak, I am asking that no harm come to these women."

"Are you begging me, Queen of Hasan Daeg?"

She swallowed hard. "Yes, I am, Aga Dorak. I am begging for their lives."

He moved closer until his lips were touching her hair. "What about the woman, Maura? Is she also begging?"

Maura closed her eyes.

Dorak laughed and pushed her away. "You win for today. I am so happy to see you up and about that I will grant your wish."

There were collective sighs from the small knot of women huddled together.

"Of course, you will have new quarters. These rooms are now officially off-limits to you and your companions."

He laughed and flicked his sword at Maura's shredded clothes. "It pains me to tell you this, my lady, but I have never seen you clean. Next time you are in my presence," he pointed to her hair and face, "please do something with yourself. It is very depressing to look at you." He smiled a rakish grin and called for the guards. "Ladies, follow me."

Maura started forward.

Dorak waved her away. "I will keep my end of the

bargain. They will not be killed or even tortured, but I am going to keep a very heavy guard on them."

He bowed very low to Maura. "You better start thinking about what you are going to give me in return for my generosity." He began leading the women out of the room.

"One more thing," Maura called out.

Dorak swirled toward her.

Just for a brief second, Maura could see deep anger welling in his eyes. "Yes, Queen Maura?"

"May I keep Lady Sari?"

Dorak looked at the old woman. "If it pleases you. I must take my leave. I have been up rather late and would like to sleep now."

"Where are the guards taking me?"

"To your new quarters. I know those rooms have no secret passages."

"And pray, where is that?"

Dorak yawned. "Right next to my chambers."

"That is impossible. It is not respectable."

Dorak gave Maura an irritated look. "Madam, do I look like I give a damn about respectability? I am going to bed. I do not wish to talk anymore. If you give my guards any trouble, they have orders to drag you by the hair of your head to your quarters. Good night!"

Dorak strode out of the room.

Bhuttanian guards entered and escorted Maura and Lady Sari to their new quarters.

As Sari hobbled after the queen, she thought about the day's events, but what bothered her were the looks that Maura and Dorak exchanged with each other. There was too much heat in them. Too much hate in their exchanges. Hate and love were opposites of the same coin. She knew the gaze of desire when she saw it.

Dorak wanted Maura to be more than just a political wife.

What caused Sari's heart to fear was that Maura wanted him too and wondered if the young queen realized it yet.

6

There was a pounding on the door.

Sari, who was sleeping on a pallet, got up and limped over to answer. Her old bones creaked as she pulled open the door.

A courier asked permission to see the queen.

Sari told him to wait in the next room, and the queen would see him when she had dressed.

The courier did as instructed.

When Sari closed the door, Maura jumped out of bed. "What does he want?"

"I do not know, but he is from Dorak. You must hurry."

Maura washed her face and dressed in a rush, but entered her private audience chamber calmly.

The Bhuttanian courier bowed in the Hasan Daegian manner and greeted her. "Salutations, Great Mother and

Queen. The Aga of Bhuttan and Emperor of Kaseri, asks me to convey his invitation to dine in the main dining hall."

"I see."

The courier blushed. It made him nervous to be near a woman so tall. All the Hasan Daegian women made him nervous.

"What else?" Maura asked, sensing another agenda.

"Aga Dorak wishes that you be properly attired, freshly scrubbed, and clean-smelling." The courier lowered his eyes.

Maura could barely contain her anger. She wished to pull the courier's silly plumed hat down around his neck. How insulting this was, especially when the Bhuttanians rarely bathed, and the Hasan Daegians washed every day.

Sari leaned over and whispered, "Aga Dorak is trying to raise your color."

"Thank you, courier. You may tell Aga Dorak that the Queen of Hasan Daeg will be pleased to have the Aga of Bhuttan join Her Majesty in *her* dining hall for the noon repast. Make sure you tell him in those exact words."

The courier silently mouthed the message as he backed out of the room.

As soon as he was gone, Sari laughed.

"I don't think it is funny," Maura snapped. "He implied that I am dirty. I'm not going."

"Oh, yes, you are little one. Dorak thinks no such thing of you. He just wants to anger you into making a mistake so he can pounce. Oh, how I would love to see his face when the courier repeats your words."

"Then be quick and prepare me a bath. Bring me some of my mother's robes from which to select. I am going to dazzle that coarse, stupid man."

Sari gave Maura a strange look but did as she was commanded. She prepared a hot, steamy bath with herbs and scented oil. The queen's hair was washed several times and ironed dry. Sari took great pains weaving flowers into Maura's hair, which had grown back in black and long after being with the Royal Bogazkoy.

After several hours of primping, pulling, and preening, Maura de Magela stood before Bhuttanian guards awaiting entrance into the dining hall. She stood regally in a white gown with blue trim. Yellow and white flowers adorned her hair, and she carried a silk hand fan with a drawing of the uultepes on it.

An old man, in Bhuttanian dress of the long tunic over trousers, shuffled out and bowed to her. "Your Majesty, Aga Dorak will see you now."

Maura swept past him and glided into the de

Magela's dining hall. She looked around the room. The last time she had been in it was on the day of her birthday celebration. Tears welled in her eyes as she stared at the chair in which her father had sat. He had been so proud and was the perfect host overseeing his guests' comforts. Her hand flew to her heart.

Chairs scraped the floor as Bhuttanian officers jumped to their feet. Each pressed a right fist to his heart, giving her the Bhuttanian salute.

"What is the matter, Your Majesty?" she heard Dorak say behind her. "Does the table not please you?"

Maura started. Why was he always out of sight behind her? She turned. "No, the room is lovely. It's just I feel very strange. May I sit down?"

Dorak motioned for a slave to bring a chair for the queen. He gazed about the room genuinely puzzled. Then his face took on a look of enlightenment. "You know it is much too stuffy to stay inside on such a pretty day. Why do we not eat on one of the balconies overlooking the city?"

"No, we mustn't," interjected Maura quickly. She did not want to be seen casually dining with Dorak by her countrywomen. They would get the wrong impression. "Why don't we eat in the kitchen?"

"The kitchen!"

"Yes, the servants have a nice room right off the

kitchen, and we could eat at their table."

Dorak hesitated.

"Are you too good to sit at a servant's table, my lord?" asked Maura, fanning herself.

"Frankly, yes, but if you want to." Dorak gave the order that they would dine in the kitchen. He offered his arm to Maura.

Politely, she took it and walked with him.

"I hope this makes you happy."

"If you want to make me happy, leave my country."

Dorak chuckled. "I want to make you happy, not giddy."

Maura smiled at him. As she walked, she noticed all of his servants had iron collars about their necks and kowtowed as the royal couple passed. "What are those things around your people's necks? They look awfully heavy."

"Just adornments, nothing more."

Maura took exception but said nothing. She needed to cultivate his good will. She was planning to ask for a favor.

Dorak spun Maura around and looked her up and down. "Your Majesty, I must say you are stunning. And I see you have changed your hair color again. But not only the hair color but the length as well. You must have a skillful hairdresser."

The officers walking behind them murmured in agreement. Maura noticed the general called Alexanee kept quiet.

Maura ignored the comments about her hair. "Thank you. This robe was a favorite of my mother's."

The grin fell from Dorak's face.

Smiling sweetly, Maura tugged at his arm and led him down the hallway.

Catching sight of Maura and Dorak entering the kitchen, the servants flew into a flurry of activity.

Dorak glowered at the Hasan Daegians as they clustered around Maura in a tight group. He pursed his lips when Maura shook hands and even hugged a few as they greeted her.

They scattered when Dorak gave them a stern look.

"I see you have been down here before," Dorak said, following a servant to the kitchen dining room.

The Hasan Daegian queen laughed. "Yes. I think I have spent a good deal of my childhood with cooks and serving maids. Most of them helped raise me. I know more than once they hid me in the pantry to escape a spanking from Lady Sari."

"I find it difficult to believe that you ever required corporal punishment," commented Alexanee.

Turning, Maura stared at the impressive-looking general. She did not reply as he had spoken without her permission. She expected Dorak to reprimand Alexanee, but he didn't.

"Of course, they spoiled me with food. So when I was home, I would come down here and stuff myself with cakes and puddings," Maura said to Dorak.

"Were you away from home often, Your Majesty?" Alexanee inquired.

Maura ignored the general's question as she sat at the servants' table.

Tall goblets, filled with wine, were brought.

Dorak sneered at the ruby liquid. "What I am in the mood for is shaybar. Yes, milk with thick foam." He slapped his hand down on the table. He leaned toward Maura. "What is your pleasure, Lady of the House?"

The Bhuttanian officers remained standing at attention.

Maura was ravenous. "I want warm bread and cakes with lots of honey icing to start."

Dorak leaned back in his chair. Addressing a trembling Hasan Daegian maid, he ordered meat for himself.

Bread was immediately put on the table, as were several jugs of borax milk.

Dorak poured a goblet of milk for Maura as well as one for himself. He took a drink, made a face, and then swallowed. "I remember now that I hate this stuff. It's too wholesome," Dorak said smiling. "My father would mix borax blood with milk or boiled water and drink it all the time. Most of the older Bhuttanians do. It is what my people once lived on."

Wiping the foam from her lips, Maura teased, "Not human blood? You disappoint me, Aga Dorak."

"We can't be savages all of the time. But when we do drink human blood, it should always be that of a virgin." He winked at the maid serving them and gave her a lecherous once over.

Maura gave him a disapproving look. "There is no need to frighten these people." She turned to the addled serving maid. "You may go now."

The girl bowed and hastily retreated behind a dark cupboard where she pulled her apron over her head.

"I thought all Hasan Daegian women were brave warriors," drawled Dorak, noting the maid's timid demeanor. He slapped butter on a hunk of bread.

Maura started to reply but thought better if it. She drank more of the milk to stall for time. She felt all of the eyes of the officers observing her, but it was Alexanee who gave her pause. She detested sharing a meal with Dorak and his men, but for the time being, she could not afford to alienate him. She would have to bide her time until she could make her next move. She looked up from her thoughts and was surprised to find Dorak studying her. "What are you looking at?" she asked sharply. Dorak always took her by surprise.

Dorak rubbed his chin. "I was just wondering how one's hair could grow so many inches overnight and turn black as night as well."

"It's a hairpiece," she lied, silently cursing for not cutting her hair to its former length.

"Is that so?" Dorak studied her intently as Maura tried not to squirm under his gaze. "Can you explain why you are not covered with puncture marks today?"

"I do not know what you mean." Maura bit into a hunk of bread Dorak had torn off the loaf for her.

Servants brought plates of steaming food and placed them on the table.

Maura eagerly began eating.

Dorak took a sip of wine from a goblet, having sent the milk away. "Last evening, it looked like you were covered with tiny wounds."

"As you can see for yourself, I am not."

"I can see that not only has your white hair grown dark in the last ten hours but your skin color is noticeably different. You were considerably paler yesterday."

"I appear darker in harsh light, just as you might turn redder."

"Where did you go last night?" asked Dorak, narrowing his eyes.

"I thought you asked me to dine, not to an interrogation," answered Maura, picking up the salt bag near his plate. She generously poured salt over her vegetables.

"As I understood my courier, it is you who invited me."

Maura took one look at Dorak's face and broke into peals of laughter. "So I did." Her laughter broke the tension at the table. She bade the officers to sit with them.

Comfortable with his men eating as well, Dorak engaged in more genial conversation. He talked of philosophers familiar to Maura.

Maura discovered that Dorak was educated. They argued over the Anqarian concept of zero, which the Bhuttanians could not fathom. Maura tried over and over to explain "nothingness" to Dorak, but he refused her explanations, saying there was no such thing as a complete void of something. She was having such an engaging time she forgot Dorak was her enemy until one of his men tapped the table to gain his attention.

"I am sorry," he said rising, "but I have matters that need my attention."

"One moment, please," Maura requested, folding her napkin.

Dorak waited for her to speak.

"I wish to pay respect to my parents."

"That can be arranged." As always, Dorak looked for signs of weakness. "Do you wish me to escort you to your parents' grave?"

Maura blanched at the thought of Dorak accompanying her to her ancestors' final resting place. Regaining her poise, she answered politely, "No, Great Aga. That will not be necessary, although you are kind to offer your assistance. I need only a small guard of Hasan Daegians to accompany me to the royal sepulcher."

For a moment, it looked as though Dorak was going to forbid Maura from leaving the palace without his guards, but he relented. He remembered the stricken look on Maura's face when she discovered the stack of corpses beneath her balcony window. He doubted she would try anything foolish, but he would have her followed surreptitiously just in case. "I will have a litter prepared for you," he said while summoning a slave.

"If it pleases you, I would like to ride my pony to my family's sacred grove. That is if my pony has not been slaughtered."

A little vinegar with the honey, thought Dorak. He smiled. "I find it very amusing that you Hasan Daegians prefer to ride your little pet ponies as though they were horses. Your feet almost drag the ground when you are astride them."

The Hasan Daegian queen returned the smile. Maura

was not going to rise to his bait. She wanted to visit her parents' grave, and she was not going to do anything Dorak could use as an excuse to stop her.

Dorak continued, "Your Majesty, I do not know if your pony survived, but if alive, it will be waiting for you in the courtyard. If it has met with misfortune, one of my horses will be given to you to compensate your loss. Now you must excuse me." He turned abruptly to leave.

Maura clutched at his sleeve.

Dorak spun around, half-expecting to encounter a dagger. He met only with Maura's pained expression.

"I sincerely thank you for allowing me to visit my parents and for their honorable burial. It is decent of you."

Dorak winced at her words. "Decency is not just a Hasan Daegian trait, my lady. Even Bhuttanians can be honorable." He stopped short and grinned rakishly at her. "At least, some of the time."

Before Maura could reply, Dorak bowed and rushed out of the kitchen with his men, leaving Maura alone.

7

Maura dressed in a white gown.

Her face covered by a blue mourning veil, she rode through the streets of O Konya in a palanquin. Her pony, Beca, could not be found, and she was wary of the Bhuttanians' warhorses.

The queen's guards, bereft of weapons, marched proudly beside her. They still made an impressive sight as they carried the royal blue banners with the crest of the uultepes on them.

Maura opened the curtains of the sedan so she could wave to the people.

The citizens of O Konya stopped whatever they were doing and ran to pay homage to their new queen. A few of the citizens spat as she passed.

Taking note of this, Maura's face did not betray her keenly felt sorrow that some of her people thought her unworthy to be their sovereign, but she could not blame them.

Her mind raced over the events of the past several months: the death of Zoar, the great Hasan Daegian victory at the border, the resurrection of the Black Cacodemon, and the fall of O Konya into the barbarians' hands. Her mind rejected the notion that there was anything she could have done to resist Dorak's dark magic.

Was the rest of her country still fighting? Without her scouts and her spy network, she was blind and deaf. She felt helpless. Still, hoping to give her countrywomen encouragement, Maura smiled and waved until she could stand it no more. Drawing the curtains, Maura shut out the light and the curious faces staring at her. By the time she reached the royal grove of her parents' final resting place, Maura had grown sullen and withdrawn. She barely looked up as she was helped from the palanquin. Ordering her guards to wait, Maura gathered her mother's ancestral sword and prayer book after accepting a small torch from one of the guards.

While following the pathway leading to the ancient sepulcher of the Hasan Daegian queens, she recited the litany for the dead. As there were no other mourners present, she read both the invocations and the responses. Feeling more despondent with each step and verse,

Maura reached the ornate marble building that housed her ancestors. She tucked the prayer book in her sleeve and ascended the steps leading into the great hall.

In the middle of the atrium were the sarcophagi of her mother and father. Traditionally, consorts were never placed with their ruling mates but laid to rest in a lesser building in the grove.

Tears sprang to Maura's eyes.

This was a great honor for Iasos to be placed here.

She realized Dorak was responsible and was grateful that he had allowed her father to be at the side of his beloved wife for eternity. Though she might have wanted to, Maura would never have defied tradition in this manner.

Dorak was immune to such observances.

A flood of tears ran down Maura's face as emotions that had been pent up for so long could now be vented freely. Maura pulled at her hair and unabashedly cried out. She tore at her veil. "Mother! Father!" she shrieked, choking over the words. Overwhelmed with her loss, she rent her mourning robe and fell to her knees sobbing. Maura pounded the sides of her head with her fists.

A hand shot out and grabbed one of Maura's arms.

Startled, Maura jerked forward and almost toppled over, but was caught in powerful arms.

"Shh, shh," whispered a male voice. "You must not harm yourself. It will do no one any good."

Maura swiftly leaned her head down and bit a tattooed hand.

The man yelped and lessened his grip somewhat, allowing Maura to bring her hands up and force her captor's arms from her. She immediately rolled to her side and viciously kicked the strange man in the gut.

The man crumpled over and fell to his knees. Though winded, he tried to kowtow and show obeisance to the queen. "Please, Your Majesty! Have pity. I was trying to save you from harm." The man placed his forehead on the cold marble floor.

Panting, Maura gathered her torn robe about her and stood over the man. She kicked him again for good measure. The stranger grunted but did not move his position. "Have mercy, Queen Maura!"

Feeling in control of the situation, Maura picked up her mother's sword and unsheathed it. She placed the sword on the neck of the man prostrate before her. "Who are you?" she demanded.

The man peered upward. "May I speak freely to the queen of the Hasan Daegians?"

"You may sit up, but move very slowly or I will kill you," Maura replied, furious that an intruder had desecrated her parents' resting place.

The man straightened his back but remained on his knees. He was deliberate in his movements, making them slow and exaggerated. Clasping his hands behind his back, he said, "My name is Prince KiKu of the Hittals, fifth in line to rule after my mother and the last surviving female heir. Along with my twin sister, I was taken to court as a hostage at the age of eight by Zoar. My sister was forced to marry Zoar when she became of age, and I was kept in the Bhuttanian royal household as a means of ensuring her obedience.

"Zoar, thinking he could control me, had me trained in the arts of secrecy and duplicity. I rose through the ranks until I was made the hetmaan, Zoar's spylord. I was put in control of his vast network, and it is through this spiderweb that I learned of Hasan Daeg. I wished to live in your land, and I entered your country as a Sivan merchant after years of careful planning and finding the secret corridor from Siva into Hasan Daeg."

"You left your sister alone with Zoar?"

"My sister perished in a hunting accident. She was gored by a wild borax bull." He paused for a moment as if remembering the incident. His face hardened, and his eyes dulled with hatred. "Because of my loathing for Zoar, I became a spy for Queen Abisola and returned to Zoar's court."

"You are my mother's secret spy in the court of Zoar?"

"Was," KiKu replied, becoming animated.

"You are the one rumored to have cut the cinch on Zoar's saddle after the battle of Anqara."

KiKu inclined his head. "The same."

"And did you?"

"Your mother gave the order for Zoar's mishap in Anqara. She thought it would either kill him or slow him down, which it did."

Maura lowered the sword. "Why that particular time?"

"My usefulness to Queen Abisola was running out. There had been too many leaks, and my absences from the court were getting harder to explain. I believed Zoar was growing suspicious and planning to assassinate me. It was a scenario of now or never."

"Why did my mother wait until the fall of Anqara to unleash you?"

KiKu cocked his head to one side. "It was a simple case of logic. If the Anqarians won, then the threat of Zoar would be over, and life would go on as before. If they lost," KiKu shrugged, "your mother would have the treasure of the Anqarian banks plus the House of Magi with which to defeat the Bhuttanians."

"She never planned on the Black Cacodemon?"

"The Bhuttanians had not used magic in over twenty-five years. There was no reason to believe Zoar would start again. He disliked magicians. But we did not count on his untimely death and that Dorak would unleash the dark wizard upon the world."

"How did you gain access to my mother?"

"Your mother liked to breakfast in the royal garden. I dressed as a gardener to gain access."

"It was that easy?" asked Maura, appalled that the palace security had been so easily breached.

KiKu gave her a quick smile. "It was for me."

"And you just ambled up to my mother's table and began to chat with her?"

"I watched for many days, approaching the table closer and closer, until the queen and her guards became used to me. One morning, while pretending to prune a sinjo bush, I flung myself at her feet and gave her a pouch that would prove my claim."

Although Maura did not believe KiKu's story, it was fascinating nevertheless. She made up her mind not to kill KiKu yet, but to listen to his story. "What was in the pouch?"

"The gold seal from the hand of the statue of Bhuttu in the temple located in Bhuttan."

Maura snorted. "Anyone could have a reproduction made."

KiKu shook his head. "There is only one seal such as this in the world. Your mother knew it was genuine."

KiKu waited for Maura to question him further but when she remained silent, he continued. "The seal can be identified in two ways. There is writing on the band that is invisible to the naked eye until heated. It also has a secret compartment known only to the senior priests of Bhuttu and, of course, to myself.

"What is in the compartment?"

"I never knew. The seal could be broken but once. Your mother had the seal opened by my instructions and read the inscription. Whatever the message was, it was enough to convince her that I was whom I said. We reached an accord. I would return to Zoar's court and act as a double agent. When my service was over, I would be allowed to return to my country and live out my days in freedom, something I had not known since a small child."

"Do you have a theory about the inscription?"

"I believe that the inscription had information concerning the fall of the Overlords at the hands of the Lahorians."

"You know of the Lahorians?" Maura gasped. This was only the second person to speak to her of the Lahorians. Iegani was the first.

KiKu nodded his head.

The mourning queen sifted through KiKu's story for inconsistencies. There were many pieces of information missing, but perhaps the spy thought he had little time and wished only to provide the highlights before they parted. "What do you want of me?" She wondered if this man had been planted by Dorak to trick her.

"Your father told me to meet you here and present you with this." KiKu handed Maura a letter.

This was the letter of which Meagan had spoken. Maura took the parchment and eagerly broke the seal.

Dearest Daughter,

It is my gravest wish that you are alive and in good health. The man who brings this letter is KiKu. He is a spy and has worked for your mother many years. It is he who caused the cinch on Zoar's saddle to tear, thus causing his accident. It gave us ten more years to prepare. He is to serve as your advisor, and you may use him as you see fit. It is the last gift your mother and I can give you.

I have not much time. I do not mind. I already miss my wife terribly and wish to join her as soon as Mekonia deems it. My only regret is that we leave you behind.

Daughter, be strong. Survive so that you may fight another day.

To prove that KiKu is as he says, he will give you a sign; the one I talked of so long ago at the City of the Peaks. I must go now. It is time. All my love.

Your Father,
Iasos

Maura wiped tears from her eyes so they would not stain the parchment.

"Is that not your father's handwriting, Your Majesty?"

Maura nodded and looked up at KiKu with tenderness. "I thank you for this."

"We must burn it."

"No!" cried Maura, clutching the letter to her breast.

KiKu was stern. "We must."

She hated to part with the letter but knew KiKu was right. The letter had to be destroyed immediately. Maura reluctantly threw it in the flame of the torch she had placed in a stand. The letter was reduced to ashes within a few seconds.

Sighing, she gently patted the sarcophagi of her parents before turning to KiKu. "What else do you have of my father's?"

KiKu slowly reached inside his dirty tunic and pulled out a crumpled piece of cloth. He handed it to her.

Maura unwrapped it and let out a small gasp. It was her father's betrothal ring that signified his status in court and his relationship to her mother. "How did you get this? My father never took this ring off."

"Your father told you that if he ever needed to get a message to you, he would send this ring."

"I had forgotten, and I had promised him that I

would not." She had to control her anger. If indeed, this man was sent by her father, she could not squander such a precious resource. "What do you propose to do, KiKu, Hetmaan of the Spies?"

KiKu resisted wiping the sweat from his upper lip. He could have killed this girl easily many times during their talk and disliked being the target of her swordplay. He realized she was the key to his dreams and that he must make her trust him. He wanted to break the Bhuttanian Empire. This young flower before him was needed to help plot against Dorak.

"The western regions of Hasan Daeg have not surrendered to Dorak. He has given these areas little attention while keeping the main part of the army in O Konya."

Maura thought this tactic strange. "Do you know why?"

"He seeks the women from the House of Magi. Dorak secretly interrogates them. Those scholars who have managed to flee the city have taken refuge in the cities west of here or with the Dinii in the City of the Peaks."

"What is he after?"

"He seeks knowledge of the Mother Bogazkoy."

Maura fell silent.

KiKu studied the young woman's blank face, which

offered no insight as to her thoughts. He sighed inwardly, knowing this relationship with this young woman was going to be trying. He did, however, admire her courage and could sense a keen intellect behind her blue-tinted eyes. KiKu thought Maura had the same strange alien beauty he had found in her mother. He needed to know if she could be as ruthless as Abisola. Maura needed to be if she were going to outwit the cunning Dorak.

Maura finally spoke. "I am allowed no contact with my advisors nor any of my staff, except for Lady Sari. I have not heard from the Dinii. I have had no messages from Iegani. If I do anything that looks suspicious, Dorak rounds up my people and executes them. How can I fight Dorak when I can't find my warriors? I am in a desperate situation."

"I can act as courier to your army and to the Dinii, but first, you must find the Mother Bogazkoy and mate with her."

Footsteps sounded on the marble stairway leading into the atrium.

Maura turned and saw several Bhuttanian soldiers coming toward her. Frantically, she spun around, but KiKu was nowhere in sight. Realizing her actions would make the soldiers suspicious, she began wailing and pulling at her hair.

"Your Majesty, are you all right?" asked a young officer wearing an elaborate metal helmet with many red plumes.

Maura looked up from beneath her tangled hair. "What do you mean by disturbing my mourning? How dare you invade my privacy? Get out! Get out!" she screamed. "I will inform Dorak of how you disturbed me during my time of grief. He will no doubt hang you for your lack of respect."

The officer's expression froze at the mention of Dorak. "My apologies. Please forgive us. We only feared that something had happened for you to tarry so long. Please excuse us for our ignorance of your ways." The officer bowed and quickly backed out of the atrium and ran down the marble steps.

Maura followed the soldiers to the edge of the steps and saw that her guards had been surrounded by armed Bhuttanians. She looked at her shamed women with disgust. "You could have at least warned me," she yelled. Deciding she would deal with them later, Maura returned to the atrium where she studied the room.

"KiKu. KiKu," she called softly.

No response came from the marble hall.

After waiting about an hour, Maura relented and left the final resting place of her beloved parents, leaving her grief to reside with them.

8

Lady Sari stood quietly.

She watched a Bhuttanian slave comb and braid the queen's blue-black hair.

Sensing that Sari wished to speak to her, Maura dismissed the slave when the braiding was finished. As soon as the door closed behind the departing girl, Maura swiveled in her chair to face the older woman. She did not give Sari leave to sit down.

Lady Sari took note of this but was determined to speak. "May I talk with you, little sparrow?" she asked, barely able to contain her frustration.

Maura nodded with reluctance.

Lady Sari squared her shoulders. "It has been many months since you have visited the final resting place of your parents. Since that time, you have been close with your thoughts. You have confided with no one. I have seen little effort being made to throw the enemy out of our country. Instead, you dine with Dorak, hunt with Dorak, talk with Dorak, and listen to music at night with Dorak. You permit Dorak to stroke your hair in public." Sari hesitated a moment out of fear but threw caution to the wind. "Do you not understand how this looks to the citizens of O Konya? Many think you are consorting with the very man who brought such unhappiness to our land?"

"What are your thoughts, Sari?" asked Maura, her voice cutting like sharp flint.

"I wish to guide you away from folly. Perhaps because you are so young, you do not grasp the significance of your actions."

"I understand exactly what I am doing," Maura replied. "Let me just remind you of who I am."

Maura rose from her cushioned chair and stood only inches from the trembling advisor. "I am your queen. It is your sworn duty to obey me in all things. If you ever question my loyalty or duty to my country again, I will have you beaten. I swear it, old woman!"

Sari's lips quivered, and her shoulders slumped with defeat. "I am sorry. I have overstepped my place. Please forgive me." She knelt as fast as her advanced age would allow.

Maura turned away and sat in her chair before a

dressing mirror. She closed her eyes briefly and calmed herself with the techniques Iegani had taught her. For the past few months, Maura had been receiving telepathic messages from him imploring her to come to the Forbidden Zone by any means possible. Lately, however, she had difficulty making out his words.

She wanted desperately to join Iegani at the foot of the Mother Bogazkoy and receive her blessings. Since she had been with the Mother Bogazkoy's offspring, the Royal Bogazkoy, she had felt the ancient Mother Tree call to her over and over again. The Mother Bogazkoy desired to reproduce and needed Maura to achieve this goal.

All Maura could think of was to get to the Mother Bogazkoy as soon as possible, but she could not even stray from her chambers without Dorak having her watched. She had not heard from KiKu and had no idea where he might be or even if he were still alive. She had to gain Dorak's trust so he would lower his watch on her. That was the only way she was going to escape the palace walls.

It stung Maura that even her old nurse and trusted companion doubted her. Still, she would not give up. She must find a way to the Forbidden Zone without implicating those near and dear to her. "Get up and fetch me some cool water," she commanded. "The morning is warm."

Sari, after bowing as low as she could, gladly left the room.

The queen looked hard at herself in the mirror. Her face was no longer that of a young woman. Her features had set and hardened. Instead of twinkling eyes, hers now glared like hard stones found on a pathway.

Dorak allowed Maura to exercise, and she worked steadily on strengthening her muscles. Her arms and legs were wiry and muscular while her stomach was flat and hard. Maura's breasts, thought ample by Bhuttanian standards, were not voluptuous by Hasan Daegian measures. Her hips did not flare out as those of the ideal Hasan Daegian female. Maura had to admit she was no great beauty as she looked in the mirror. Her tinted blue skin only added to her alien look.

She wondered what Dorak thought as he looked at her. Did he desire her? Or was she simply someone he must endure on the way to securing the Hasan Daegian throne? Maura sighed.

Her thoughts went back to long summer evenings spent with Chaun Maaun under a brilliant star-lit sky. She missed him pleasuring her body. Wondering if he was well, Maura's head drooped as memories of passionate lovemaking spilled over. Would she ever know tender moments like that again? Maura purged such thoughts from her mind.

She could not afford to wallow in the past if she was going to deceive Dorak. Dealing with Dorak required all of her concentration.

A sharp knock at the door broke Maura's thoughts. She bade the person to enter.

A slave crossed the room bearing scarves for the queen to select for the day's apparel. The woman was unknown, and this immediately put Maura on guard. Her brow knotted, thinking the new slave might be a spy placed by Dorak. Yet, there was something familiar about the woman.

Maura studied the slave while pretending to select one of the muted-colored scarves. The woman was too tall to be a Bhuttanian but was too flat-chested to be Hasan Daegian. Finally, it came to her. "Good morning, KiKu," Maura whispered.

The slave raised her eyes, and the corners of *her* mouth turned slightly upward. "I think Your Majesty will find this scarf suitable for your ride today," said KiKu. *She* held out a scarf to Maura, who reached for it. "You must hold it to the light in order to see the intricate pattern," recommended the slave.

Maura did as instructed and held the scarf up to the window. Inside the scarf's design was a message written in Anqarian script.

She returned the delicate material to the servant. "I do not think so," she replied, picking up a muted blue and green silk scarf. "You may go now," she ordered the servant. "I have what I need."

KiKu bowed and gave Maura a knowing look. He silently quit the room, passing undetected by the guards at Maura's door.

A few hours later, Maura found herself riding on a Bhuttanian warhorse in the forest behind the palace.

The very size of the Bhuttanian mounts had, at first, caused Maura concern. But once on the broad back of one of the mares, Maura relaxed as she realized the mare's temperament was not at all different from her beloved pony. She liked riding high on the beast's back as she went through a series of exercises to determine the animal's capabilities.

Though powerful and sturdy, the Bhuttanian horse could be outmaneuvered by the smaller Hasan Daegian ponies. It was more difficult to redirect the massive bulk of the Bhuttanian warhorse quickly.

She thought of uses other than war for the animals. These robust steeds could till fields all day and never fatigue. Maura made a mental note to discuss the possibility of a breeding program with Dorak.

At a reasonable distance behind the queen rode her guards on their small ponies. Behind them trotted

Bhuttanian soldiers assigned to make sure the queen was safely delivered to Dorak, who was overseeing work on a new aqueduct he wanted to show Maura.

Riding deep into the forest, Maura twisted and turned her mare among giant fern trees and briar patches. Looking back, she found she had eluded her guards. Giving the horse a vicious kick, she spurred it into a meadow. Galloping at full speed, she heard the Bhuttanians call after her in the distance. Kicking her horse even faster, Maura dropped the reins around its neck, took her feet out of the stirrups, and lifted her arms about her head.

A whoosh sound came from above, and Maura was lifted into the sky. She glanced at the talons clutching her. They were of a red Dini hawk. A warrior. It could only be Yeti.

Maura relaxed as the Dini wound skillfully through the dense foliage in the forest and came to rest on the strong limb of a mingo tree.

Yeti placed Maura carefully on the broad limb.

Hearing the familiar click of the Dinii language, Maura slowly sat down as instructed. Looking about, Maura saw Yeti confer with another red hawk who she knew to be Iegani's apprentice.

The Dini hawk approached Maura. She bowed low and said, "Greetings, Great Mother, Maura de Magela, tenth ruler of Hasan Daegian, Healer of the Infirmed. I was sent by the Great Divigi to speak with you."

Maura brightened at the mention of Iegani. "Greetings to you, Toppo. What news have you?" She ignored the fact that Toppo had remained standing and was towering over her. This was against Hasan Daegian protocol.

"I see the Hittal was successful in getting to you our message."

"Yes, KiKu is most ingenious, but I do not need to tell you that my absence is most dangerous. If I am missing very long, Dorak will start rounding up citizens and killing them."

Toppo's narrow face relaxed. "Ah, that explains much." Toppo sat on her haunches so she was eye level with Maura. "May I, Great Mother?"

Maura gave Toppo permission to sit.

The red hawk paused for a moment while chewing on some mingo leaves.

Maura could tell Toppo was gathering her thoughts. She waited politely as the Dinii often took a long time between sentences. The Dinii were a precise race and wanted to get every nuance perfect to explain their meaning. When dealing with the Hasan Daegians, the Dinii took longer than usual as they were speaking in a second language.

This fact notwithstanding, Maura needed to move this meeting along. "Do you wish to speak in Dinii?" she asked.

Toppo nodded. "My master, Iegani, wishes to know why you do not come to the Mother Bogazkoy."

Maura was taken back. She was not in the habit of explaining herself, and it was the second time this morning she had been confronted by those making demands on her intentions. She reflected on the implications of the question. "Answer this first, please. Why has Iegani stopped communicating with me? I have not heard from him for many days."

Toppo smiled, exposing her large teeth stained with yellow mingo juice. "My master has been communicating with you every day. Since he has not felt your presence, he thought you might be terribly ill or that . . . "

"Or what?" questioned Maura, growing impatient.

Looking uneasy, Toppo replied, "He thought that perhaps you might have learned to stop him from communicating with you."

The queen pursed her lips. "Why would I do that when I am dying to learn some news? Dorak has cut me off. I can get nothing out of his servants. Bhuttanians simply do not gossip with Hasan Daegians," explained Maura, exasperated with her situation.

Toppo bowed her head. "My pardon, Great Mother. I can see now Iegani has been thwarted by the Black Cacodemon. Even the Lahorians have been trying to reach you telepathically."

"Lahorians!" cried Maura.

Toppo realized her mistake in mentioning the Lahorians and steered the conversation away from them. "I was sent to tell you that you must come to the Mother Bogazkoy. Her cycle to reproduce is almost finished. Without you, there is no hope, and without her, there is no way you can shield yourself from the magic of the Black Cacodemon." Toppo stated emphatically again. "You must come!"

"I cannot," Maura pleaded. "If I leave, Dorak will start killing my people in retribution."

"The few must be sacrificed for the good of all."

Maura was horrified. "Surely, you do not mean that. So many have died already."

Toppo's ears perked. "The soldiers are coming. There is not much time." The red hawk extended her hand to help Maura rise. "You must find a way to come to the Forbidden Zone soon. You have only three cycles of the moon left." Toppo fixed her steady gaze on the queen. "You must come! There is no other way." With those words, she spread her wings and flew away.

Yeti jumped down and, with an extended talon,

began ripping Maura's clothes.

"What are you doing?" exclaimed Maura.

"We must make it look like you fell from your horse. When I put you down, make sure you rub dirt on your face," advised Yeti.

Satisfied with Maura's tattered appearance, Yeti picked up the queen and flew her to the ground, allowing Maura to fall with a hard thud. Yeti flew back to the tree and blended in with the branches.

Even Maura with her keen eyes and tracking ability had a difficult time discerning the Dini's location.

Bhuttanian soldiers reeled into the meadow. The warhorses came bearing down on the queen with such speed that, for a moment, she wondered if they would be able to stop without trampling her first. The horses pulled up several feet short of Maura, causing her to let out an audible sigh of relief. She tried her best to look rattled, which was not hard to do.

An officer jumped off his great stallion and knelt by the queen. "Your Majesty, are you all right?" he asked, trying to keep the exasperation out of his voice.

"I think so," Maura replied timidly. "I could not control my horse, and I fell off—as you can see." She pointed deep into the forest. "I think he went that way."

The young officer looked skeptically at the queen. He knew what an accomplished horsewoman she was, but she made a convincing sight with her torn clothes and dirty, sweaty face. However, she should at least know the difference between a mare and a stallion. His eyes scanned the forest for possible intruders.

"Can you help me up?" asked Maura innocently.

Reluctantly, the officer tore his eyes away from the dark, intimidating woods patched with silver mist and was secretly glad the Hasan Daegian queen had been thrown in a meadow. Bhuttanians were from the wide, open steppes and considered forests unnatural places. He helped the young woman stand.

As Maura placed weight on her feet, she winced from pain. "I think I twisted my ankle during the fall."

The officer knelt and examined Maura's legs. "It does appear that your left ankle is swelling."

At this time, the Hasan Daegian Honor Guard rode into the meadow. Angry that the Bhuttanian soldiers reached their charge first, the women could barely hide their contempt as they jumped off their ponies and pushed the Bhuttanian men aside. "We will take care of our queen," said the highest-ranking Hasan Daegian.

The Bhuttanian officer, wishing to avoid a confrontation with the women, bowed to the queen and asked permission to withdraw.

Maura nodded.

He saluted the Hasan Daegian officer in Hasan

Daegian fashion and got back on his horse. "I will leave six of my men to help escort your queen to O Konya. I will send back a litter so that it might ease her journey."

The Hasan Daegian guards glared at the Bhuttanian as he rode off with several of his men. One of her women asked, "Great Mother, do you think you can ride?"

Maura nodded.

A Hasan Daegian officer brought her pony over and helped the queen on. Walking beside the animal, the officer turned it toward O Konya and began the long trek home.

Dorak's aqueduct would have to wait.

Maura dared not look in the trees but could feel Yeti's eyes upon her group. Determined to comply with the Mother Bogazkoy's wish, Maura knew she had to escape to the Forbidden Zone.

The question was how!

9

Maura waited patiently.

She sat with her hands folded in her lap as Dorak paced angrily before her. She stifled a yawn. By now, she was used to his ranting and was fairly confident she could persuade Dorak to see things her way. Her calmness only served to make Dorak more furious.

"I do not believe your horse threw you. I personally selected a very gentle mare."

"Even the best horses have bad days. She threw me as I said. I am not used to handling such a large animal," defied Maura, looking straight at Dorak.

Dorak snorted in disbelief. "I find it hard to believe that you could not handle this horse, let alone one of the more spirited stallions."

Maura smiled inwardly at the compliment. "I was thrown as you can see for yourself."

"How can I tell if you are bruised with that blue skin?"

She pointed to the darker places on her arms. "Look here. You can see the bruises."

Dorak stomped over to her and peered down at her arms. He unexpectedly grabbed Maura by the shoulders, pulling her out of the chair. "If you are lying to me, you'll be sorry," he warned.

Maura caught her breath at the dark menace in Dorak's voice. She pushed him away. "I am sick of your threats. Go ahead, round up the entire city, and kill them all. I do not care anymore. You treat me like one of your slaves. I am not allowed to speak to anyone. I do not know what is happening outside this city. It's driving me crazy, you understand!" she screamed at Dorak. She fell back into her chair, sobbing.

Dorak, surprised at her ferocity, gently touched her shoulder. "Did you meet anyone?" he asked quietly.

Maura shook her head adamantly. "I did not meet any of my people or yours in the woods," she answered truthfully.

Dorak studied her for a moment. "I believe you," he said. He pulled up a chair and straddled the seat. Dorak lifted Maura's chin.

Tears streaked her face.

He pulled a handkerchief from his pocket and wiped

away her tears. "Here," he said, giving her the cloth. "Blow your nose. You look awful."

Maura took the handkerchief gratefully.

Suddenly, Dorak leaned over and kissed Maura softly on the mouth.

Startled, Maura pulled away.

"Don't," he said quietly. "Maura, I am not like my father. I will not lay waste to lands just because I can. I want to build a great empire with roads and cities that are centers of learning and trade." He gently touched her cheek. "I do not want to kill anymore. I want to build."

Dorak moved closer to her. "Do you not see that the two of us could create a wondrous civilization? We are alike, you and I. We are cut from the same cloth." Dorak's eyes took on an intense, dreamy look. "Believe in me as I believe in you."

Maura stared into Dorak's black eyes and felt herself slipping into them. "This cannot be," she said, resisting his pull. "We can never be on the same side. We are enemies. You defeated me, and my honor will never permit me to forgive you."

Dorak took her hand and began lightly kissing her fingers one at a time. "An honorable person knows when she has been defeated fairly and to accept the situation."

"But you did not defeat me fairly," hissed Maura, her fingers tightening hard around Dorak's hand. "You used evil magic which even your father refused to seek."

Dorak kissed Maura's thumb and took it into his mouth.

Maura drew in a sharp breath and exhaled slowly. Her eyes closed.

"Then meet me on the field of battle, just you and I," cooed Dorak. "If you win, I will leave Hasan Daeg. If I win, you will become my wife of your own free will." He kissed the palm of her hand with light, flickering touches. His face was crimson with passion. Dorak pulled Maura toward him and held her in his strong arms. "Tell me your answer."

Maura seemed dazed.

Dorak shook her hard. "Tell me, woman!"

"No tricks?"

Dorak held up his hand to his heart. "Upon my honor as a Bhuttanian."

Maura felt her heart quicken.

"I want to be more than your liege lord, my gracious queen. I want to be your husband. I want to be your partner as we build a world of grace and beauty."

"What are the rules for the combat?" asked Maura.

"Hand to hand with any weapon you choose."

"Until death?"

Dorak laughed and released Maura from his hold. "No, my queen, only until one corners the other. There will be no death with this fight. I will not kill you, and I hope you will return the favor."

"If I fight, I will try to kill you," Maura said defiantly.

Dorak's brow furrowed. Disappointed, he stood back from her. "As you wish. Try to kill me if you can, but I am going to win and make you my wife."

"And I am going to win and regain my throne."

"You have your throne already, and with my help, you can gain the throne of the world."

"I will have none of you," Maura spat.

Dorak raised his hand as if to strike the rebellious woman, but dropped it harmlessly against his side. "Be stubborn, Maura, but I will win, and you will be my bride!" He stomped out of the room.

"Tomorrow at noon in the courtyard," Maura called after him.

Dorak slammed the door after him.

Even through the thick wooden door, she heard him cursing down the hallway to his rooms.

Maura ran into her bedchamber where Sari awaited and fell at her feet.

Sari stroked Maura's hair. "I heard, little sparrow. You must not fight him. If he wins, you will lose your honor."

Maura looked up at Sari through her tears. "If I win, he will be dead, and I will have freed my country."

"Then why do you cry so much? I heard him say he will not kill you in this fight. He has already given you a great advantage. The both of you are about the same height. It will be an evenly matched contest. You can kill him easily."

Maura hid her face in Sari's lap, mumbling something.

Sari lifted the queen's face. "I cannot hear you."

Maura's eyes had a wild look of despair. "I said I do not want to kill him. I want him to live. I have feelings for him." She shuddered with shame.

Sari wrapped her arms around Maura, rocking her gently. "I know this. I think he has feelings for you too. That is what makes this situation so awful."

Maura was momentarily lulled by the familiar comfort of Sari's arms. She closed her eyes and let Sari soothe her. "Tomorrow, I will kill Dorak and all of this will be over," Maura whispered.

10

Dorak waited.

Dressed in black, he waited for the Hasan Daegian queen on the cobblestones in the courtyard. He wore a red strip of cloth around his dark hair. It was hot, and already he was sweating. He ordered chalk and dipped his hands into a bag that a slave brought. *Where is that woman?*

The courtyard was empty except for Alexanee acting as his second and one slave boy.

Bhuttanian soldiers and officers hid in the recesses and windows of the courtyard, as did their Hasan Daegian counterparts, to cheer on their champion.

Maura stepped into the courtyard wearing black as well with gold uultepes embroidered on the back of her shirt. She wore a leather vest with braces on her forearms, and her head was shaved.

Dorak gaped at Maura's bald head. He silently cursed her for pulling a stunt that threw his concentration off. Dorak also admired her for doing so and wished he had thought of something so visually startling. For the first time in many months, Dorak thought he saw a ghost of a smile on Alexanee's face.

Seeing Dorak's confusion, Maura threw him a big grin. Behind her walked Sari, who was in turn followed by Rubank carrying a blue pillow. On the pillow lay two immaculately polished swords. Maura halted before Dorak and bowed.

Dorak returned the gesture.

"If it pleases the aga, Consul Rubank has chosen two weapons he finds satisfactory for combat." Maura waved Rubank forward.

Rubank held the weapons for Dorak's inspection.

"I hardly think the word combat is correct for betrothed persons such as ourselves. I would just call this a lovers' tiff," replied Dorak, winking at Maura.

The soldiers hidden in the walls' recesses laughed out loud while the Hasan Daegians twittered.

Maura pretended not to notice Dorak's brashness or hear the laughter.

Alexanee picked up one of the swords and inspected the blade. "Both weapons seem in splendid condition. If I may, I would prefer this one for Aga Dorak," he said, slashing the sword through the air. "The balance seems better."

The sword whizzed near Maura's ear, but she did not flinch. "If we might start, Great Aga," she said sweetly. "I would like to dispatch you before my noon meal."

Alexanee seemed astonished at Maura's boldness. He looked questioningly at Dorak.

Dorak merely gave her a rakish smirk. "The only thing that will be killed today, Queen Maura, is your arrogance." He looked about him. "I feel like a victor."

"So do I," replied Maura, stretching her legs.

Dorak bowed again and turned to practice with his sword.

Maura continued stretching her taut muscles, keeping a close eye on Dorak's movements. She nodded that she was ready and signaled for chalk to be poured into her hands.

Sari handed her a towel, and Maura wiped sweat from her face.

A cloth similar to Dorak's was placed on Maura's head. Out of the corner of her eye, she saw something white flutter in the breeze. She turned sharply and observed Meagan the Healer sitting with a Bhuttanian soldier guarding her. Meagan looked paler and thinner but otherwise seemed fine. She sat beside her medical bag and gave a small wave.

Maura sighed with relief.

Dorak had kept his pledge.

Maura understood the appearance of Meagan. It was Dorak's way of saying that he had honored his promise, and he did intend to marry her. Maura shuddered both with pleasure and horror at the thought of becoming Dorak's wife. Realizing she was losing *her* concentration, Maura silently cursed Dorak and searched for him.

He was lounging against a railing, studying her.

Rubank went to the center of the courtyard. He bowed to his queen and then to the aga, motioning both of them to come near him.

Dorak was not familiar with the dueling statutes of the Hasan Daegians. He could find nothing about warfare in the royal library and was suspicious that this was the first duel in centuries. Maura was probably making up the rules as she went along. The Bhuttanian way was far simpler. Each opponent stood at opposite sides until a horn sounded and then rushed toward each other until one was dead.

Dorak masked his anger when Rubank searched for hidden weapons on him. When Rubank finished, Dorak motioned for Alexanee to search Maura.

Maura stood expressionless as Alexanee patted her down. He even had Maura take off her boots so he could look at the bottom of her feet.

Sari stamped her foot at General Alexanee's

impudence.

When finished, Alexanee merely grunted to Dorak.

Maura motioned for Rubank.

The consul knelt on all fours behind the queen so she could sit on him while Sari helped her with the boots. Now ready, the determined queen picked up her sword and balanced it in her hand. She nodded to a servant, who rang a centuries-old bell that was suspended above the entryway.

Upon hearing the bell, all Hasan Daegians left their tasks and went into the streets. Facing the palace, every Hasan Daegian woman, man, and child knelt and began praying to Mekonia, their nature goddess.

Curious, Bhuttanian soldiers and Sivan merchants followed the Hasan Daegians into the streets watching the seldom seen ritual of Tsnsuni.

The Bhuttanians asked the Sivas in the Anqarian language if they knew what was happening.

The desert merchants shrugged their shoulders and replied they had never witnessed such a sight before.

While the Bhuttanians were taken back by Hasan Daegians kneeling in the streets, the Sivans became bored and lumbered back to their caravans or taverns.

The Bhuttanians stayed and watched. They knew fervor when they saw it. This was something they had in common with the Hasan Daegians.

11

The wizard opened his greenish eyes.

Feeling a shift in the atmosphere, the Black Caco-demon rose from his pallet only to don black gloves over his pale skin. A fine dust rose up from his parchment-like flesh as he moved.

Sensing something was happening, the wizard left his dark, narrow room in the cellar of the palace and hurried to the roof. There he saw thousands of Hasan Daegians kneeling to pray. He stretched out his arms, testing the air only to find he did not like the vibrations.

Hurrying to the other side of the roof, the wizard peered down. There he saw the Hasan Daegian queen and the Bhuttanian aga ready to engage in a duel.

Why was he not informed of this? Anger shot up the wizard's spine. What fool thing was Dorak doing?

He would have to stay in the burning sun and watch,

making sure the little Hasan Daegian witch did not harm Dorak. The young aga was too important to his plans.

Dorak and Maura stepped into the middle of the courtyard.

Rubank held up a blue and gold scarf.

The rulers crossed swords.

Maura never took her eyes off Dorak's, which seemed blacker than ever.

Rubank dropped the scarf.

Like lightning, Maura spun around and brought her sword to Dorak's head.

He parried, just barely missing the blow.

Acting as the aggressor, Maura pummeled Dorak with blow after blow.

Dorak avoided being struck by the sharp edge of the sword.

Maura sliced his clothes, nicking his skin. Moving to his left, Maura stepped out of his range. "Why are you not striking back?" she cried, lowering her sword.

"I am too damned busy trying to keep my head intact," Dorak yelled. "Here I come," he cried, running toward her. At the last moment, Dorak veered off to the side and hit Maura on the buttocks with the broad side of his sword. "As I said before, your death by my hands is not my intention," cooed Dorak, leaning on the sword hilt with his feet crossed. He gave the stunned queen an arrogant smile.

Maura was speechless. She felt fury rush over her face. "How dare you insult me like this," Maura hissed. "Come back and fight!"

"I bow before your prowess with a sword, my lady. You possess as much strength as two men. I do not remember you being this strong when last we fought. Perhaps you have had communion with a spirit . . . or a magical tree."

He shifted his feet. "It might interest you to know, my little Hasan Daegian treasure, that I surveyed the caverns beneath the palace.

"It took me days, but my men found a huge underground lake with an island. On this barren island, they found debris of a rotting plant. My best men examined it, and they tell me that the dead thing has remnants of Hasan Daegian hair and blood on it. Now, don't you think that is interesting? A plant with human blood. Blue blood, that is. Well, it has all sorts of interesting implications." Dorak blew the queen a kiss.

Maura did not charge the boasting aga but stood her ground. She knew Dorak had succeeded in making her too angry to fight effectively.

Iegani had taught her that angry warriors make dead warriors.

She scanned the courtyard with her peripheral vision, placing everyone. She wanted to make sure some assassin did not sneak into the courtyard and kill her with an unseen dagger while Dorak taunted.

The Black Cacodemon, realizing that Maura would spy him, touched a medallion on his chest, causing him to become invisible.

Maura remained stationary as Dorak circled her. Without warning, she advanced upon Dorak with stunning speed.

He barely had time to lower his sword before she was thrusting at him. Dorak turned and parried too late.

Maura had pushed her sword into his side.

Grunting with pain, Dorak reached down and felt his side. His hand was bloody. Dorak looked at Maura in disbelief. "You have cut me to the bone!" he cried out bewildered.

Maura raised her sword to make the final blow. Convinced of victory, Maura started down with the sword. She would make Dorak's death quick and painless.

Suddenly, the avenging queen felt a ball of intense heat descend upon her shoulders as though the sun had exploded. She cried out in surprise more than pain. The heat became so intense Maura dropped her sword and fell to her knees. She held her hands over her eyes to shield them from the blinding light.

Dorak, clutching his bleeding side, hovered his sword over Maura's neck. He deftly nicked her and watched the blue blood ooze from her skin. Angry, Dorak kicked Maura's sword away from her. Hearing someone plead for Maura's life, he turned and saw Sari begging on her knees. With his sword still at Maura's neck, he raised his face to those assembled. "Before all present," Dorak shouted, "before the rules of combat, I claim this woman to be my wife. She will marry me at the time and place deemed proper by me. If she refuses to honor her oath, then she, with her kith and kin, shall die by Bhuttanian custom."

Dorak dropped his sword and began to wobble. Feeling the world spin about him, Dorak was unconscious before hitting the ground.

Both Bhuttanians and Hasan Daegians ran to their rulers.

Meagan of Skujpor pushed everyone out of the way and began administering to the fallen warriors. She applied a compress to Dorak's side and instructed Alexanee to maintain pressure on the bandage.

Turning Maura over, she gasped. Maura's face and hands were scorched with large, angry blisters forming while other parts of her skin were seared as though she had been roasting on a spit. "The queen has been burned! Quick, we must get her out of the sun. Hurry! Hurry!"

The soldier who had been guarding Meagan helped Rubank carry the Hasan Daegian queen to the kitchen, the nearest set of rooms off the courtyard.

Dorak was carried by Alexanee.

Both of them were placed on tables in the kitchen where Meagan's initiates had scattered the cooking implements on the floor. As soon as Dorak and Maura were put down, the women went to work cutting off the their clothes.

Alexanee chased the servants out of the kitchen and placed guards at the doors. He silently cursed himself for allowing this duel to take place, but the general had not taken it seriously. Believing that Maura would not have the courage to harm Dorak, he dismissed her. He knew that Dorak's fondness for this woman would restrain him.

He had underestimated both their passion and de-termination to win. Even if they both survived, the fact that a foreign man had cut their queen would not sit well with the Hasan Daegians. And there was the question of how the queen became burned.

To all appearances, Alexanee seemed collected when he gave the orders for martial law, but his heart was racing so fast he thought he might faint.

If the Hasan Daegians rose up in rebellion, the Bhuttanians would quash them, but Alexanee would be battling an uprising thousands of miles from home with several hostile countries lying between him and Bhuttan, cut off from reinforcements and all communication. With odds like that, only a small percentage of his men would ever see home again.

Sari stayed outside in the courtyard with Alexanee's officers investigating the walls and recesses. She saw nothing to explain Maura dropping her sword when victory was so near. Believing something unnatural had happened, Lady Sari searched the courtyard, finding nothing out of the ordinary. She swore, though, as did the Bhuttanians warriors, that she could hear a distant laughing.

12

Maura sat up.

She was in a makeshift bed located in the kitchen. The fire in the great stone fireplace, where gleaming kettles hung and meat for the Bhuttanians roasted on spits, was out. The bustling kitchen staff, in their blue aprons dusted with flour and netted turbans wrapped around their heads, was absent as well. Only nervous guards and busy healers were in attendance.

Too bad the Dinii did not know of this moment. It would be the perfect time to strike.

Looking over to the other side of the room, Maura spied Meagan bending over Dorak. Seeing him bloodied, Maura winced and let out a small moan.

Sari, who had been sitting in a wooden rocker by the queen's cot, awoke from her fitful sleep. "Your Majesty, you have awakened," said Sari smiling. "I will get

Meagan."

The young woman shook her head. "There is no need," Maura replied, prying off bulky bandages from her arms and hands.

Sari tried to stop her. "You mustn't! You have been burned."

"I was burned, but am no more."

Sari shot her a disbelieving look.

"Truly, I am healed. Help me, and you may see for yourself."

Lady Sari gingerly unwrapped the queen's bandages. Opening her mouth in astonishment, Sari exclaimed, "I see nothing! The Bogazkoy, though dying, still gave you much power." She turned Maura's hands over and peered closely at the skin. "There is not even one scar. It is a miracle! Mekonia be praised!"

"What's this on my head?" asked Maura, fingering goop that had been plastered on her face and scalp.

"An ointment of Meagan's for burn injuries."

"Hand me a towel."

Sari hesitated.

Again, Maura reassured her. "My face will not be burned as you see my hands are not."

Sari handed her a kitchen towel which Maura took and vigorously rubbed the heavy ointment off her face.

Maura turned her head for Sari's inspection. "What

is happening?" Maura asked, looking toward the healers at a large table on which Dorak lay.

"Dorak is dying. You struck him a fierce blow before you fell."

"I must not let this happen. Help me up. I must go to him."

"Let the dung-eater breathe his last. He has brought us nothing but unhappiness. With his death, we shall be free again. Isn't that what the duel was about?"

"I cannot let him die now. His people will say that he won fairly. The Bhuttanians will accuse us of some foul complicity and go on a campaign of retribution. His people will see his death as murder, not from an honorable duel. If only he had fought me in earnest instead of playing. The Bhuttanians have taken all of our weapons. We cannot defend ourselves. I must save him!" Maura swung her legs around the side of the little cot. Her head felt woozy, and her legs were unsteady.

"Look what he did to you. He did not win the contest fairly. If he does not die, you will have to marry him. Please, let him join his dead father," Sari pleaded.

"He did not harm me. I am sure. Tell me, did you see anything? A strange light?"

"It was very odd. You were starting to bring down your sword to deliver the deathblow when you just went down. Nobody could understand why you fell. It was only after we turned you over that we saw the burns. The air felt so hot we could barely stand it."

"But not around Dorak?"

"No, little sparrow."

"And you saw nothing?"

Sari shook her head.

"And you heard nothing?"

The loyal servant paused for a moment. "I lingered outside searching for clues and to make sure the Bhuttanians did not tamper with any evidence. I saw nothing out of the ordinary, but thought I heard a strange squealing sound. It was very high-pitched. It sounded almost like laughing to me."

Maura reflected on Sari's words for a moment. "I have no doubt he was laughing."

"Who, little sparrow?"

Maura ignored Sari's question. "Tegani was right. I will have to be with the Mother Bogazkoy before I can face the Black Cacodemon. He is too powerful for me."

Sari gave the little band nursing Dorak a black look. "I want him to die."

"Dorak must live for now. Help me to him."

Meagan of Skujpor, hearing whispering, turned and saw the Hasan Daegian queen rising. Flustered, she ordered the Bhuttanian guards, "Put that woman back!"

The queen's guards, who had been watching their

sovereign and Sari from the corner, sprang up ready to sacrifice their lives.

Maura ordered, "Stand aside."

Her guards parted and fell in beside her.

Maura pointed at the Bhuttanian soldiers. "If you dare touch my person, I will have you killed as is my right. Now out of my way."

The confused Bhuttanians looked at Alexanee.

Stress lined Alexanee's face.

If they touched the Hasan Daegian queen and harmed her, news of it would spread throughout the city like wildfire. This towering woman may not be as popular as her beloved mother, but she was still revered by the population. The reports of Hasan Daegians praying in the streets proved that. The general motioned for the Bhuttanians to step aside.

Leaning on Sari, Maura went over to Dorak. She sensed the Bhuttanian soldiers were placing their hands on their swords as she approached their aga.

Meagan bowed as did her initiates. "Great Mother, you seem to have recovered," she commented with one eyebrow raised.

"Is that your apology for ordering commoners to touch the Royal Queen of Hasan Daeg?"

Meagan's green eyes, red with strain and worry, blinked once and then boldly made contact with the strange blue ones of the Hasan Daegian queen. "If it pleases you, you may take my life when this little drama is over."

Ignoring her remark, Maura asked, "Dorak?"

Meagan wiped her forehead with a clean towel. "You struck him in the side. It missed his major organs but I cannot stop the bleeding. I think he is hemorrhaging inside."

"And?"

"If I cannot stop the bleeding, he will be dead in a few hours," Meagan replied with finality.

Maura looked at the Bhuttanian physician assisting Meagan.

He nodded in concurrence.

Taking a deep breath, Maura declared, "I can save him."

The Bhuttanian healer protested vehemently.

The soldiers drew their swords while Maura remained very still.

Meagan motioned for everyone to be quiet.

Turning to Alexanee, Maura appealed to the stone-faced general. "It is well known that Hasan Daegian queens can heal when it so moves them. Look at me. Was I not covered with burnt flesh? I have healed my own skin. My skin is as normal as yours." She held her arm out to Alexanee.

"It could be a trick," cautioned a Bhuttanian soldier.

"Quiet, you cur," ordered Alexanee, chastising the outspoken warrior. The bedeviled general asked the Bhuttanian physician, "What is your opinion?"

The healer shook his head in amazement. "These people show wonderful recuperative powers. I have read their medical texts in detail. There are recorded stories of Hasan Daegian royalty saving those who are even in worse condition than our aga. There is historical precedent. Whether this queen can," he bowed in deference, "I do not know. But her burns should not have healed for many months, and there should be evidence of heavy scarring."

"What do you have to lose?" Maura asked. "He is going to die anyway. I might be able to save him."

Alexanee looked at Meagan.

Meagan nodded her head, and then looked at the Bhuttanian physician, who concurred.

Alexanee walked over to a window and looked out. He was quiet for a long time. "Why save him when you tried to kill him?"

"If the aga dies now, your soldiers would decimate my country before returning to Bhuttan. They would do so because they would think he was murdered instead of perishing in a fair contest of arms. And you would be the one to give the order, thus consolidating your power. But all the Bhuttanian generals would be vying for power, and there is a good chance you would be assassinated on the way home."

Alexanee pondered her words. Finally, he spoke to Maura, "If you fail, you will die."

"I accept your condition."

"Great Mother, do not do it. He's not worth it," Sari begged.

"The aga must live, Sari," replied Maura, pushing the woman's pleading hands off her arms.

Meagan moved out of the queen's way but stood where she could watch.

The Bhuttanian physician tiptoed beside her.

Alexanee stood by the window, his shoulders heavy with tension. He gave Maura leave to proceed.

Maura bent over Dorak and studied his face. His mouth twisted from suffering. "Dorak. Dorak," she called.

"Can you hear me?" She gently wiped the grime from his brow. "I am going to place my hands on your wound. You will feel heat. Do not fight it. Blend with it. It is healing and will make you well." Maura placed her hands carefully on his wound.

Dorak moaned at her touch.

Alexanee's hand tensed over the hilt of his dagger.

Maura closed her eyes and concentrated. She felt a

strong surge of energy come from deep within her bowels and move through her spine. It flowed up through her arms and out of the palms of her hands. A glowing light emanated from her fingertips and melted into Dorak's flesh.

Dorak turned his head, crying out.

"Do not fight it," whispered Maura, "or we shall both be dead."

Dorak relaxed at the sound of her voice and lay still. The light emanating from Maura's hands became stronger and brighter.

Everyone moved back as sweat poured off Maura's face. She felt a towel wipe her face. The sweat on her arms sizzled and hissed as it rose as steam. Maura lost herself in the healing of Dorak. She began to feel her consciousness merge with his. Frightened that she would lose herself, Maura pulled back and hurled herself from the table, hitting her head on the flagstone floor and was dazed for a moment.

Several hands reached down to help her up but pulled back after touching her scorching flesh.

A chair was brought. Maura fought back nausea as she rolled to her knees and pulled herself up on the wooden chair. Smoke rose where her hands touched the wood. Standing uneasily, Maura caused her mind to dampen the blinding light, and as a torch that runs out of oil, her inner light dwindled until it was extinguished.

Squinting, Maura saw several of her guards examining their hands.

They looked at her in wonder.

"It feels wonderful!" one exclaimed.

"It both warms the skin and soothes. I can't describe it," a guard muttered to Meagan.

"Yes," confirmed another. "It feels like . . . youth."

Unsteady, Maura hobbled over to Dorak's table again. She glanced over the Bhuttanian physician's shoulder as he busied himself examining Dorak's wound.

"I do not know what Her Majesty did," the physician said to Alexanee, "but this wound has stopped bleeding. I see signs of healthy tissue already growing back." He turned to Maura. "If you were not the queen, I should like to study you."

Alexanee, relieved that he was not going to have to issue an order for the annihilation of the Hasan Daegians, pushed the Bhuttanian doctor out of the way. He examined Dorak. The aga's color had returned, and his pulse seemed strong. Alexanee had seen enough battle injuries to recognize a healing wound.

Dorak's eyes fluttered open. The first person he saw was Maura peering down anxiously at him. "I told you that you would not be able to kill me," he said huskily.

"I did my very best," replied Maura chuckling.

Everyone joined her.

Dorak's puzzled look only caused more laughter. He was very suspicious that the joke was on him, but he did not care as he had won the hand of the Hasan Daegian queen in marriage. The secret of the Bogazkoy could not be very far behind.

Lady Sari sensed a strange presence in the room. Looking behind her, she caught a fleeting glimpse of a black-robed figure descending one of the staircases leading to the cellars. She shuddered at the recognition. She remembered looking out her window the night of the invasion during the battle in the courtyard and seeing the Black Cacodemon fluttering over dying Hasan Daegian warriors waiting for the moment of their deaths.

How long had the Black Cacodemon been watching?

13

Maura rested.

At dusk, she rose from her bed.

With the help of young noblewomen acting as servants, she bathed and dressed in a simple green robe with a woven hem dyed light blue.

At Sari's insistence, Maura ate only a light dinner of fruit and bread. Afterwards, she sat on her balcony overlooking O Konya.

A servant lit incense, and a young boy, sitting in the corner, played the lute softly.

Citizens of O Konya were already lighting their oil lamps for the coming evening. The city twinkled and shined like a precious gem.

The air smelled sweet while distant mountains rumbled like a hungry gootee. Rain was coming.

Lulled into deep meditation, Maura pondered on the

terrible war and the cost that Dorak had inflicted upon her people because he needed to feed his own. Could he not have accomplished this with trade?

That had not been good enough for Zoar or Dorak. They were men who needed to dominate women, treasure, land, water, objects that fed their insatiable lust for power. Otherwise, these men would drown in self-doubt.

Maura became aware of someone listening to her thoughts. She created an aura of protection about her mind to lock out the intruder . . . a simple trick Iegani had taught her. This procedure left her disoriented for a few seconds. Maura pinched her earlobes so her senses would clear. She scanned the palace walls searching for anyone who might be spying on her. Seeing no one, Maura studied the boy musician.

Feeling the queen's gaze, the boy stopped playing and looked up at her with large, questioning eyes.

Deciding that he was just a little boy with a gift for playing the lute, Maura smiled.

The boy relaxed, returning to his strumming. He had thought his playing had displeased the queen and that his ears were going to be boxed for it.

Finding no evidence of an intruder in her chambers, Maura could only surmise that the telepathic interloper had been the Black Cacodemon. She scowled at the thought of the dark-hearted magician.

He had seldom appeared since the invasion of O Konya, but Maura was quite sure he had ventured into the light to cause the sea creature to attack at the underground lake and to produce the mysterious burns during the duel, even though Dorak denied that the wizard was still in O Konya. Maura pondered what to do. Squaring her shoulders resolutely, Maura left her chambers to see Dorak.

In the hallways, she had to raise her skirt to avoid debris strewn about by the Bhuttanians who were in the habit of throwing their trash wherever they stood. There were fruit rinds, dirty cups, parchment scraps, and muddy boot prints on the wide marble corridors.

Maura noted that the hems of costly tapestries were filthy from being used as towels or handkerchiefs. She tried not to show her disgust and wondered if much of O Konya was still as beautiful as it was before the invasion. Or were the Bhuttanians slowly turning the garden city into a sty as they were the palace?

Since Dorak's compartment was next to hers, Maura reached it quickly and stood patiently as Dorak's guards searched her for weapons under the watchful eyes of her honor guard. Both sets of soldiers eyed each other with contempt.

While the Bhuttanian men still regarded the female

Hasan Daegian guards as nuisances, they had acquired a begrudging respect for the tall women who so zealously protected their sovereign, even though they might only use their hands as weapons. The Bhuttanians had curtailed their abuse of the female guards since discovering that these women would do more than slap faces when offended.

More than one Bhuttanian warrior had found his nose bitten or his ear torn off when he had acted aggressively. These Hasan Daegian women were not submissive like their wives at home.

The Bhuttanians opened the massive doors to Dorak's chambers and let the Hasan Daegian queen enter.

A slave showed the queen to Dorak's bedchamber, and there she found him sitting up in bed, sipping broth from a cup held by a Bhuttanian slave girl. The girl wore the Bhuttanian traditional low-cut tunic over pants. Her dark, lustrous hair was undone and hung down her back instead of being in the usual braid worn by the Bhuttanian women. Her feet were bare and jangled with the many brass ankle bracelets she wore.

Upon seeing Maura, Dorak dismissed the girl.

She bowed low.

Maura was sure that from Dorak's vantage point, he was able to see all of the girl's assets. She wondered if the slave did more for Dorak than just feed him. She felt a stab of jealousy and was surprised by it.

"Your Majesty, how nice that you honor me with your presence," Dorak declared.

Maura returned his smile and was happy that he seemed genuinely glad to see her. "I have come to discuss the wedding," she said mildly. She pointed to a chair. "May I sit?"

Dorak pushed maps and reports out of the way, making room for her on his bed.

Another slave scurried to pick them up and left the room.

The aga patted the bed. "It is very nice here," he said grinning. "It will strain my neck if you sit farther away."

Maura sat on the edge of the bed and spread her skirts about her. "I see your bandages are smaller. You must be healing nicely." She sniffed the air. "No stink of infection."

"I'm doing rather well. I must thank you formally for not finishing me off."

"Not every day is perfect."

"I hope all of our arguments are not so costly," uttered Dorak smiling, "or so painful."

"Once married, I doubt we shall speak at all."

"Why would you say that?"

"You will be returning to Bhuttan."

"I have no intention of returning to Bhuttan, and if I did, you would go with me."

Maura gave Dorak a charming smile. "Once married, you will have the key to Hasan Daeg. You need not stay, and why would you? The Bhuttanian Empire is immense. Hasan Daeg will become just another small fiefdom paying tribute to the Bhuttanian aga."

"There is you," replied Dorak, lowering his bedcovers, thus revealing a muscular chest.

Maura almost broke into laughter. Men were all alike, forever playing the coquettish bed toy.

"Besides, I like it here," continued Dorak. "I might make O Konya the new seat of my government."

Maura bristled at the last comment. "That is ridiculous. We will marry, we will bed, and then you will return to your homeland."

Dorak put his hands behind his head. "You make it sound like such a cold arrangement."

"Our marriage will be a political arrangement. That is all!" snapped Maura, weary of his sexual posturing. She wanted him to put some clothes on.

"It doesn't have to be."

"Surely you jest. What else can there be between us?"

Dorak began playing with the fabric of her skirt.

Maura jerked it out of his hands. "Perhaps I should

call your slave girl back. You seem in need of a cold bath."

"Why should I call her when you can give me one?"

Maura snorted with anger. She turned away from Dorak.

"Don't be angry. You might not want to please the aga, but would you please your husband?" Seeing that Maura was still offended, Dorak changed the subject. "Let us discuss the wedding."

"Hasan Daegian couples marry before all their kith and kin."

"As do Bhuttanians," replied Dorak, wondering where the conversation was going.

"Yes, but the Hasan Daegian couples do so naked," said Maura with a straight face.

Dorak could not keep from laughing and held on to his wounded side. "You do not, little liar. Besides, it would take more than standing naked in front of a bunch of old ladies before I would pull out of this wedding."

Maura smiled. "Well, we do invite all of our kin, and I would expect that we observe my customs of marriage since you are marrying me in my country."

Dorak looked suspiciously at Maura. "There is a lot of me and mine in that statement."

"It is the bride's wishes that are followed, not the

groom's."

"I see. What if I elect to follow Bhuttanian customs?"

"It will be as you wish, Great Aga, but you are too good a politician to realize that doing so would greatly displease the Hasan Daegians you now rule, not to mention your future wife. You do want to make me happy, don't you?" Maura fluttered her eyelids.

Once again, Dorak burst into laughter. "You almost kill me to win your freedom, and since you've failed, you are trying another tact." He grabbed Maura and kissed her firmly on the lips.

Maura liked the musty smell of him and returned his warm kiss without thinking.

"You are a wonder. What children we shall have."

Blushing, Maura pushed him away. She was not used to Dorak's rough handling. Chaun Maaun had always been gentle.

Still, Dorak's touch electrified her while Chaun Maaun's had merely soothed her like a warm summer shower. Passionate images of coupling with Dorak rose in her mind. She found herself studying the black hair on Dorak's chest. It had been a long time since she had been with someone, and she missed being touched.

Dorak let his finger wander down Maura's neck and chest until it came to rest between her breasts. Her cleavage felt warm and moist. He gently removed his finger and sucked it.

Maura took a sharp breath.

Leaning toward her, Dorak's eyes became heavy with desire.

Maura placed her hands over his encroaching arms and held them firmly. "Give me the wedding I desire and what is due to me as queen of Hasan Daeg."

"You shall have it," growled Dorak, "but you must be ready for me. Whatever I want, you must give to me without question."

Maura returned his heated gaze boldly. "I understand."

Dorak shook her. "To understand is not enough! You must want me!"

The young queen felt the blood rush to her face. "I will want you, Dorak, and all that comes with you."

"I want you to wear a gown of white without blemish." Dorak's hands began to roam Maura's body. He touched her breasts and kneaded her stomach. His breath became labored. "I do not want you to bathe before I come to you."

He grabbed her hair and pulled her face closer. "Your hair must be worn loose." Dorak leaned forward, kissing her cheeks. He then bit her lips lightly.

Maura kissed him back roughly.

"What else do you want?"

"Can you love me?"

Maura drew back. "Love?"

"Is that too much to ask?"

Maura bowed her head in confusion. She never once entertained the idea that Dorak would want love.

Disappointed by her response, Dorak hid his feelings. "We will take it one step at a time. I feel tired. Please go now. Make the arrangements as you wish."

Maura rose from his bed and moved toward the door. Stopping, she turned. "Dorak?"

"Yes," he murmured, his head already on the pillow.

"Do you think you could love me?"

"Who will have time for love when one is ruling an empire?" Dorak responded, hoping to hurt her as she had just injured him.

Maura quietly left the room. Tears welled in her eyes, but Dorak did not see them.

He was staring at the ceiling when the door closed. "Yes, I could love you," he whispered to no one in particular.

14

Maura fumed.

A conclave of administrators, military personnel, and advisors sat around the royal dining table squabbling about the correct protocol for the royal wedding.

Bhuttanians sat on one side fuming, while the Hasan Daegians sat on the other, glowering at their queen.

Maura had long since abandoned the idea of making the Hasan Daegians and Bhuttanians sit next to each other.

The Hasan Daegians, a particular and fussy people, could not stand the crudeness of the warring Bhuttanians who blew their noses on their shirtsleeves and freely spat on the carpets.

To show their disdain of the conquering nomads, the Hasan Daegians had come with perfectly combed hair decorated with flowers and immaculate flowing gowns of elegant designs.

The Bhuttanians arrived in full military dress with their weapons prominently displayed.

The Hasan Daegians, seeing the Bhuttanians swagger into the dining hall with their daggers and swords, immediately badgered their queen to dismiss with the proceedings altogether.

To avert disaster, Maura firmly replied that the Bhuttanians were merely showing respect by wearing their dress uniforms and weapons. War was all they knew, and their entire culture and protocol were built around it.

This explanation did little to soften the Hasan Daegians attitude toward the Bhuttanians. As far as the Hasan Daegian women were concerned, their queen was being forced into an undesirable marriage with a brute. Their only hope was that one day the Bhuttanians would be thrown out or, at the very least, the offspring from this hated union would blend both cultures together. They did not even guess that perhaps Maura secretly wished for the marriage, that her feelings for Dorak were deep and complex, and her heart raced upon seeing him.

The Bhuttanians were confused by all of the fuss. The verbal abuse from the Hasan Daegians did little to make the Bhuttanians agreeable, even though most of them did not understand the Hasan Daegian language. They did, though, understand the gestures the women used. It only stiffened their resolve not to negotiate with women at all. "Where are your husbands?" they demanded in Anqarian. "We must negotiate with the men in charge!"

Maura slammed her fist down on the table. "THAT IS ENOUGH!" she commanded in Anqarian, the universal language. "You have been in this country long enough to understand that our men are homemakers and do not handle matters of state."

The large, gruff Bhuttanian men snickered at this, but with a very stern look from Alexanee, the smirks quickly disappeared from their faces.

The queen turned to the Hasan Daegian women and spoke in their language. "You must stop this constant arguing with the Bhuttanians. They don't understand it. You must show them respect."

Maura slowly rose from her chair so her words would have more impact. "Aga Dorak and I wish this wedding to take place a week from now with all honors befitting a royal marriage. If we are disappointed, we are going to identify those who have wronged us, and the punishment for our displeasure will be of the same severity for both Bhuttanian and Hasan Daegian. Do I make myself clear?" She repeated her warning in

Anqarian and Sivan.

Both the Hasan Daegians and Bhuttanians nodded or murmured their acquiescence.

Alexanee motioned for a servant to come to him. With great deliberation, he unsheathed his sword and handed it to the servant with orders to place it by the entrance. He then gave a stern look at his subordinates. Reluctantly, the other Bhuttanians stood and removed their various weapons and threw them in a pile by the main door.

Everyone knew the Bhuttanians kept several knives in their boots, but the Hasan Daegian women were diplomatic enough not to mention this.

The women were pleased and would no longer hold up the negotiations. They understood the symbolic gesture of the Bhuttanians and gave their queen the signal to proceed.

Matters of food, invitations, and flowers were discussed.

The Bhuttanians, not knowing the fine art of Hasan Daegian weddings, kept silent during the lively discussion.

Whatever the Hasan Daegian queen wanted was fine with them. It was only during the subject of security that the Bhuttanians became animated. No Hasan Daegian warriors would be allowed to accompany the queen nor guard the palace. The matters of security were to be entirely in the hands of the Bhuttanian army.

"What if Mikkotto tries to assassinate me during the wedding?" Maura fumed.

The Bhuttanian officers, including Alexanee, merely shrugged. They were concerned with the safety of the aga and would permit no armed Hasan Daegians near him.

"Without my personal guards, my safety is compromised."

The Bhuttanians took offense, and their backs straightened in their chairs.

"Your Majesty," Alexanee said. "We shall protect you as one of our own during the festivities."

The angry queen dismissed his remarks with a wave of her hand. "We all know that Mikkotto infiltrated the Bhuttanian ranks before and made traitors with some coin. I want my own guards."

The officers' faces reddened at the implied insult.

"You say you do not know where Mikkotto has fled. She could be enjoying sinjo tea with the Black Cacodemon at this very moment for all I know."

Not rising to the queen's bait, Alexanee stressed, "With as many people as you are inviting, our security must be tight for your sake as well as our aga. We simply cannot allow armed Hasan Daegian soldiers, who have not pledged their oath of loyalty near Aga Dorak!"

"DO AS SHE COMMANDS!" boomed a voice from the doorway. In strode Dorak wearing a flowing grey cape with a black lining, his hair glistening from rain droplets.

Maura knew he had been exercising one of his great warhorses.

Everyone immediately jumped to his or her feet except for Maura.

The Bhuttanians pressed their fists to their chests while the Hasan Daegians merely inclined their heads.

Maura shot a warning glance at the Hasan Daegians. They reluctantly gave stiff little bows.

"I have come to find my bride-to-be and discover her entangled with a bunch of petty bureaucrats who are wasting her valuable time with nitpicking and complaining." Dorak gently placed a hand on Maura's shoulder. "I wish the pleasure of your company for the noon meal."

"Your wish is my command, Great Aga," replied Maura, pleased at his touch.

"I would make this suggestion," advised Dorak, glaring at the audience still standing. "Form committees and have them make recommendations by tomorrow. Once you have decided, they will be responsible for carrying out your plans, or we shall carry them out feet first the day after the wedding. I wish to be the only one who monopolizes your time."

Maura had been trained to lead through a more diplomatic process than Dorak. However, she could not deny that such blatant threats had a very quick and mobilizing effect on the intended. She always took note of how Dorak handled his violent and stubborn men.

Lady Sari, who had been standing behind the queen's chair along with Rubank, approached Dorak, "Great Aga, may I speak with you?"

Dorak had long taken note that Sari, though of no official capacity, was of great importance to the royal family. Her advice was sought by the young queen. This alone made the woman important to Dorak.

At his command, a chair was brought for Dorak. Motioning to Sari, Dorak gave her leave to speak freely.

"When Queen Abisola was married, I was greatly involved with the wedding and oversaw many of the details myself. Of course, I was younger then, but I think I could still do it."

Dorak had not expected Lady Sari to offer her help and glanced at Maura.

The blue-skinned queen sat quietly, but her face was frozen with fear. He knew immediately that Maura had no prior knowledge of Sari's offer. "Why would you wish to help with this wedding since we all know of your feelings regarding me?"

Sari blushed to the roots of her tidy white hair. "I have not changed my opinion. However, Hasan Daegian queens mate for life, and if this wedding occurs, you will be our king. My thinking is that if you are pleased with the wedding, you will treat the queen well, and your heart will soften toward the Hasan Daegians who are under your control."

Dorak pondered her words as Maura stirred uncomfortably in her chair. "Has my reign been that awful for the Hasan Daegians? Your possessions have not been stolen. Your children have not been sold into slavery. The population goes about its daily life largely untouched by my soldiers."

"I am an old woman. I have nothing to lose by speaking my mind."

"There is your life."

"My life, for all intents and purposes, is over. I am living on borrowed time and know it."

"Then speak freely as long as your words are not treasonous."

"Great Aga, it is true that our buildings are being rebuilt to their former glory. Families have not been torn apart. We are not starving as is much of the world. Life in the city goes on as it had before the invasion. However, certain leaders of our community have disappeared, never to be seen again, such as the women from the House of Magi."

"They simply fled O Konya."

Maura stirred and tried to gain Sari's attention.

"I do not accept this," Lady Sari replied in a bold tone. "I have heard rumors that they are being detained by Bhuttanian soldiers somewhere in the city."

Dorak rose from his chair and faced Sari. "Are you calling me a liar, old woman?" Dorak asked, his voice sizzling like water over hot coals.

Maura prayed that Sari would tread more softly.

Sari smiled sweetly. "Of course not, Great Aga. I am merely suggesting that you may have forgotten where you put them."

Dorak started to speak and then halted abruptly. His gaze moved from Sari to Maura's amazed countenance until he threw back his head, laughing. "You may not like me, Lady Sari, but I like you very much indeed. I wish I had twenty diplomats like you. I would not need an army."

Dorak bent forward and kissed Sari's withered hand. "You may indeed be in charge of the wedding. Do as you please as long as it satisfies my intended bride."

He turned to Maura. "I will give you your wedding present now, my love. All detainees from the war will be set free on the day of the wedding, even those corrupt women from the House of Magi. I am sure I will be able to remember where I have put them by then."

Maura slid out of her chair and kneeled before Dorak. "Thank you, Great Aga. This is most gracious of you."

"I do not understand your strange attitudes toward war. Prisoners are taken all the time, and nothing is thought of it."

"That is until you have been taken prisoner yourself," replied Maura, looking up at Dorak with a sour smile on her face.

15

Maura appraised herself.

She gazed into a large standing mirror in her chambers at her blue and gold wedding gown trailed by a sheer white train encrusted with pearls. Her black hair had grown back and was held in place by a simple circlet of white rooshars, a rare marsh flower. She wore her mother's emerald signet ring, which was now hers as ruler of Hasan Daeg. On her feet were dainty gold sandals. A blue gem-encrusted belt encircled her narrow waist.

Maura despaired when she saw that her maid had applied too much makeup. Not wanting to hurt the girl's feelings, Maura sent her for some water. After the maid left, Maura patted her face lightly with a damp towel. Too much makeup on her blue skin gave Maura a bizarre appearance. Satisfied, Maura turned toward Sari who hurried into the room, limping and using a cane.

Alarmed, Maura bade Sari to sit and helped ease her into a chair. "Is all ready?"

"All is in readiness, Your Majesty," informed Sari, wheezing.

"You seem out of breath."

Sari held up her hand. "I will be fine."

"You should not run at your age."

"The hallways seem longer these days, and my feet swell," complained Sari, good-naturedly pointing to her cane. She clapped her hands together in glee. "Little sparrow, wait until you see everything. It is all so beautiful. If only your mother were here."

"I do not think she would want this for me," lamented Maura, thinking sadly of her mother.

"How stupid of me!"

Maura patted her on the knee and got pillows on which to rest Sari's swollen feet. "It should be a happy day."

"How can it be happy when you are marrying someone you do not love? Hasan Daegian queens always marry for love. That is one of the reasons they live so long."

Maura laughed. "Is it? I was always under the impression that it had something to do with the Royal Bogazkoy."

Sari raised her hand up to her lips. "You must never say that out loud. Dorak has spies everywhere."

"You think Dorak does not know about the Bogazkoy? I know that within days after my visit with the Royal Bogazkoy, he found its remains and knew everything there was to know about it."

Sari moaned. "Why him?"

"It could be worse. It could be Zoar who would be my groom today. At least Dorak is handsome and intelligent. He is also sensitive." Maura paused for a moment. She started to fiddle with the hairbrush on her dressing table, not wanting to look Sari in the eye. "Maybe I can bring him around to my way of thinking."

"Do not think for one moment that you could ever tame Dorak. He is a wild thing, a law unto himself. Even his own people don't understand him. They say he is strange because he is only half-Bhuttanian. I will grant you he has been good to our city, but we do not know what he has done in the countryside. He may have destroyed entire towns and villages."

Sari looked bitterly at Maura's reflection in the mirror. "We are blind. We have no knowledge of the outside world." The flesh on Sari's face stretched with anger, giving her skin a puckered look that was unbecoming. "Dorak can never be trusted. Never!"

Maura looked at Sari's reflection in the mirror. Sari's

eyes cast a weary look. "I know," Maura sadly replied to her. "He is the enemy, and I can never trust him."

A knock sounded on the door. It was abruptly opened by a Hasan Daegian guard.

A Bhuttanian escort guard stepped inside. A young officer dressed in his nomadic finest marched smartly up to Maura and bowed very low. "We have come to escort you, Great Mother," he announced gravely.

Maura followed him into the hallway where stood the marriage palanquin. At the poles supporting the chair were two Hasan Daegians accompanied by two Bhuttanians. All looked approvingly at the young queen, who studied the decorated chair.

"Does it please you?" asked Sari anxiously.

Maura smiled. "Yes, Lady Sari. It is lovely."

Sari's wizened face broke into a radiant beam.

Maura approached the palanquin and touched some of the hundreds of blue and yellow flowers so expertly woven on its structure. The poles were wrapped in gold foil. Fragrant aroma wafted on the gentle breeze throughout the hallway, which Maura inhaled deeply. The scent was glorious.

"Hurry," Sari cautioned. "We do not want the flowers to start wilting." She helped the queen step into the lovely wedding chair.

"Your mother had one just like this to carry her to

the binding ceremony," she said absently-mindedly.

"Thank you," said Maura, close to tears.

Sari pulled a handkerchief out of her sleeve and discreetly gave it to Maura.

"I have nowhere to hide it," Maura said.

"You will not need to. I will be by your side," Sari replied, putting on her ceremonial robe. She motioned for servants to pick up the gilt poles.

Both Bhuttanians and Hasan Daegians picked up the litter on cue and did not jostle the bride.

The queen's guards automatically fell into place by the palanquin. They were attired in full dress uniform of blue with gold trim. Their weapons had been restored to them by Dorak for the day and hung proudly by their sides.

Behind the marriage palanquin marched the Bhuttanian guards hand-picked by Dorak. Each member of the guard knew that this was the most dangerous time for the queen. There were both Hasan Daegians and Bhuttanians who did not wish for this wedding to occur.

The fact that an assassination attempt had not yet been made only increased Dorak's anxiety that someone would strike at Maura as she was escorted to the ceremony.

Hundreds of guests had already filed into the palace.

Dorak waited expectantly in the antechamber behind the large court hall where the wedding was to take place.

Couriers ran back and forth relaying the status of the queen's progress to the wedding hall. Three couriers had come back with good news.

So far so good, thought Dorak.

Maura had only five more hallways to negotiate.

Dorak grunted and continued his pacing, his dark eyes marking his pensive mood. He must marry this girl. It was vital to his plans. Feeling a draft in the room, he turned and watched Rubank, Maura's advisor, approached him.

Rubank seemed to glide like a silent apparition in his long maroon robe with the crest of the Bogazkoy and the uultepes on it, but then Rubank was always quiet. The royal consul was the only official position in the queen's court to be open to Hasan Daegian males.

Dorak did not understand how a person could advise when he couldn't speak, but then he thought all Hasan Daegian customs strange.

Rubank bowed. Standing patiently with his hands folded across his beautiful robe, Rubank waited for the aga to address him.

Dorak always found Rubank irritating, so he decided to have a little fun. "Rubank, how nice of you to join my officers and me. Have you come to wish me good fortune in my marriage?"

Lacking a sense of humor, Rubank had learned to endure Dorak's jesting. All Bhuttanians were great jokesters and loved to slip a marsh bloodsucker in someone's bedroll or unbuckle a saddle cinch. It seemed that for something to be funny to a Bhuttanian meant that someone needed to scream, gasp for breath, or fall off a horse.

Dorak loved to play with the hidden meaning of words.

Rubank understood that Dorak wished to catch him in his crosshairs. If he did wish Dorak good fortune, Rubank could be cited as a traitor, for this was going against official Hasan Daegian policy. If the consul did not wish Dorak good fortune, then he would displease the aga, which might cost him his head. Desiring to do neither, Rubank raised his eyebrows, indicating that he did not understand the question. He would continue with this gesture until Dorak tired of his game.

Seeing Rubank's reply, Dorak realized that he would not be able to trick the cagey diplomat today, so he opted for the true nature of his visitation. "Do you bring word from your mistress?"

Rubank nodded.

"Does it concern her location within the palace?"

Rubank nodded.

"Is she ready for the ceremony to proceed?"

Rubank nodded.

"Is she safe?"

Rubank nodded.

"Should we start now?"

Rubank nodded.

"Is there anything else you were ordered to communicate?"

Rubank shook his head.

"You may go," replied Dorak, hoping that his headache would depart with the royal consul. Slipping into an outer chamber, Dorak had his appearance checked again by his valet and then followed the High Priest of Bhuttu into the great throne room.

Hundreds of guests waited in anticipation.

Many of the Bhuttanian nobility, summering in Kittum, had arrived that morning. Most had balked at Dorak's instructions that all Bhuttanians wash before donning their finery. Yet, there they grimly sat, bathed and perfumed, next to Hasan Daegian women and their smaller husbands. Many of the Bhuttanian nobility gawked openly at the sturdy, muscular women with the voluptuous figures who did not cower before their blatant stares.

In turn, the Hasan Daegian men discreetly peered over their fans at the Bhuttanian women who were of similar stature. The females, covered from head to toe, were dark with small, trim figures. They looked older than their Hasan Daegian counterparts as they lived outdoors most of the time in harsh weather and did not have the custom of applying soothing creams to their skin at night.

Some of the younger Hasan Daegian men were intrigued by the petite women, but the older Hasan Daegian men concurred behind their decorated fans "not enough to mount."

For good measure, the Hasan Daegian women, most of whom had served in the war against the Bhuttanians, glanced at their counterparts' thick thighs and taut buttocks. They wondered how it would feel to run their cheeks across a hairy chest instead of trying to run a sword through it. More than one Hasan Daegian female closed her eyes, hoping to think of less taxing subjects.

After all, the Bhuttanians were the enemy. Still, being squeezed so tightly in a room with them was more than some of the Hasan Daegian women could bear.

More than cultivating their crops, the Hasan Daegians liked to make love and were considered by the Bhuttanians to be very hedonistic. Lovemaking was a favorite pastime, and all lovers were treasured. Many Hasan Daegian women instinctively knew they would not be cherished in return by Bhuttanian males, and this thought cooled the ardor of numerous Hasan Daegian females.

Without fanfare, Dorak assumed his place on the dais as he had rehearsed many times before the previous day.

The guests stood. Only the very old or the infirmed were allowed to sit as was the Hasan Daegian custom.

With a slight nod of his head, Dorak acknowledged the audience's obeisance. Turning to the High Priestess of Mekonia, he bowed deeply.

The High Priestess regarded him with frosty detachment.

Trumpets sounded, and the main doors were flung open. A cool breeze entered the hall just ahead of the queen's palanquin.

Delicate flute notes floated on the very breeze which now cooled the wedding guests. As was custom, the bride's litter proceeded through the center of the throng.

This part of the ceremony caused Dorak pause. He, along with many guards, scanned the audience looking for anyone with a weapon. After several tense minutes, the marriage palanquin emerged from the crowd without incident.

Dorak relaxed as guards brought the palanquin up the steps and onto the dais. Deeply inhaling the sweet fragrance of the litter, he watched as a Hasan Daegian guard helped his future bride to her feet.

Maura de Magela, tenth ruler of Hasan Daeg, looked striking as she stepped gracefully from the palanquin.

Sari, dressed in gorgeous finery, helped arrange the long sheer train on the steps.

The palanquin was removed to where Sari stood along with the Hasan Daegian Honor Guard.

Bhuttanian soldiers moved to Dorak's side.

Each group of guards turned toward the audience, scanning for trouble.

As Maura approached Dorak, she noticed his eyes were glimmering like black river pebbles in shallow water.

Reaching for Maura's hand, Dorak turned to the High Priestess of Mekonia.

Maura did not hear what the High Priestess said nor the words Dorak repeated. She did not recognize her voice responding. She saw her hands moving slowly toward Dorak to place a flowered wreath on his head.

All she heard was the voice of Chaun Maaun calling to her from a distant place. Perspiration broke out on Maura's forehead. Her limbs felt cold and useless. Chaun Maaun! Chaun Maaun! She was betraying him!

She was not being forced into this marriage. Perhaps as a queen, but not as a woman. Maura blinked back her tears.

Would Chaun Maaun ever understand? How could he understand something that she herself did not? Feeling Dorak's firm hand on hers, she looked up to see his concerned eyes searching her face. Maura gave him a reassuring smile.

Dorak turned his attention to the High Priestess once more.

The peal of the great bell resounded, acknowledging that Maura and Dorak had been married according to Hasan Daegian law and custom.

The High Priestess of Mekonia retreated to the back of the dais.

The High Priest of Bhuttu and High Priestess of Bhutta stepped forward.

Maura braced herself for the ceremony to follow.

Sari moved up the dais and removed the train of the dress, exposing Maura's back.

Beautiful backs of Bhuttanian women were considered desirable and thus shown to gain honor for the groom.

Maura's skin had been oiled and glistened in shafts of light from the morning sun.

The Bhuttanians murmured appreciatively.

The queen's back was straight, even, and without blemish except for its strange tattoo.

Sari held up the de Magela ancestral fan denoting their royal station and snapped it shut.

Maura closed her eyes as she heard the clicking sounds of fans closing one after the other throughout the great hall. She was glad Dorak did not understand the significance of the gesture which meant extreme disapproval.

Hasan Daegian women did not humble themselves to honor men. Some of the Hasan Daegians were dabbing their eyes. It was a sad day to see their queen marry outside of her people.

Maura was aware of the commotion her bare back was causing. She tried to focus her attention on Dorak, who was removing some of his clothing.

He took off his shirt and donned a ceremonial vest. She noticed how dry his olive skin was, even though it was hot.

The High Priestess spoke in the Bhuttanian language.

Maura tried to concentrate on the proper sequence of movements in which she had been coached. She repeated words she did not understand after which the Priestess handed her a sharp knife. Maura's hands were shaking as she reached out for Dorak's arm.

Dorak covered her hands with his left one and guided the knife to his wrist. "Be calm. Let me guide you."

Grateful for his intervention, Maura let Dorak guide the blade across his wrist, which made a shallow cut and dropped the knife on a pillow held aloft by the priestess.

Drops of blood seeped from Dorak's arm.

Feeling woozy in the stifling room, Maura glanced about the hall. Weren't the windows open?

She caught Lady Sari's eye.

The Hasan Daegian advisor with her elaborate hair and beautiful gown looked calm and composed. She didn't seem to be suffering from the heat. Sari gave her a quick wink.

Out of the corner of her eye, Maura saw Dorak take a similar knife from the High Priest. Hearing Dorak ask for her arm, she turned, but his voice sounded muffled and far away. When she did not respond, he gently lifted her arm from her side.

"Just a few minutes more," he cajoled. "Then it will all be over."

Maura jerked as she felt the knife nick her skin. Looking down, she saw blue blood drip onto the floor.

The High Priest said something to her, and Maura extended her arm to Dorak.

The Great Aga placed his bleeding wound over hers, and the High Priest of Bhuttu bound their wrists together with a leather cord. Then the cord was cut.

Maura knelt as she had been instructed, and Dorak

stepped back a few paces.

According to Bhuttanian custom, brides were to crawl to their husbands as a symbolic gesture of their total supplication and their husband's dominance over their lives.

After moving one knee, Maura remained still as if made of stone.

Dorak could see fury twisted across his bride's face.

Tension gripped Maura's entire body.

Dorak knew the proud queen would never come to him this way. With quick intuition, Dorak realized that Maura had been pushed as far as she was capable. She would not be humiliated before her people.

Dorak's mind jumped about for a solution. Without the last part of the ceremony, his people would not accept the marriage as legitimate. Dorak decided to do the only thing he could. He fell to his knees and crawled toward his shivering bride. Holding out his arms, Dorak whispered to her, "Come to me as I come to you."

Maura moved toward Dorak without thinking. She quickly covered the distance between them and fell into his arms.

Dorak cradled his new bride for a moment and then helped Maura to her feet.

The ceremony was over. They were married to each other according to both Hasan Daegian and Bhuttanian laws and traditions.

Feeling relieved, Maura felt Dorak kiss her on the cheek as they both turned to face a stunned audience.

Never had a Hasan Daegian queen knelt before any consort, and neither had a Bhuttanian groom crawled before his bride. Both Hasan Daegians and Bhuttanians were appalled for different reasons.

Only the Bhuttanian women were secretly pleased. They hoped that Dorak and Maura's marriage would set a precedent for their daughters' weddings. Maybe they could save their daughters from the servitude they had suffered under their demanding husbands.

At Dorak's signal, the great gong sounded.

The hands of the High Priestess trembled as she placed a crown on Maura. She waved her hands over Maura's head mumbling incantations that warded off evil. From beneath her robe, she produced a gnarled wand made from an ancient yagomba tree with which she sprinkled holy water. "Behold, these two are joined as husband and wife, which only death can sever."

"Which only death can sever," rejoined the Bhuttanians.

A gong sounded within the palace and bells heralded the marriage to the general population standing outside in the streets.

Dorak turned toward his bride. "I promised you that

once we were married, I would set free all political prisoners in O Konya. This very moment, they are being released."

Maura's face lit up as she touched his arm. "Thank you," she replied gratefully.

Smiling broadly, Dorak cried in Anqarian, "As I have taken a Hasan Daegian bride, it is my wish for my people and hers to become one. There is no longer Hasan Daegian or Bhuttanian. We are one. To signify our desire for both peoples to become united, I not only take this woman to be my wife but my empress as well. She and I will rule over our people, and one day, our child, of both Bhuttanian and Hasan Daegian blood, shall rule over a united kingdom! So be it!" Dorak led his bewildered bride back to the center of the dais.

There awaited the High Priest of Bhuttu with a crown that resembled a bull's horns carved from gold and onyx.

The High Priestess of Bhutta brought out a similar crown.

The High Priest placed his crown on Dorak's bowed head. Taking a vial of blood from his robes, he held it over the royal couple. "This is the blood of Bhuttu, who in human form sacrifices his life with the eternal copulation of Bhutta," he cried out. The priest, in his costly robes of gold, carefully opened the vial and poured a small drop of blood in the center of his palm. With his index finger, he smeared a design onto his hand. "As Bhuttu sacrificed himself, Bhutta breathed everlasting life into his nostrils." The priest smeared blood on Maura's forehead and then on Dorak's. "From your joining must new life spring."

The Hasan Daegians stood quietly as they were not sure what to make of the unexpected coronation.

Maura's eyes swept past a beaming Dorak and over the cheering Bhuttanians.

The Hasan Daegians were quiet, but she could see the glimmer of hope in many of their eyes. If their queen were empress of the Bhuttanian Empire, she might have influence over the political process that controlled their country. One by one, the Hasan Daegians realizing this advantage, patted Bhuttanians on the back and clapped their hands together.

For the first time in over a year, Maura began to feel a surge of joy. There was hope where there had been none before. She felt giddy and wanted to dance. Maura turned to Dorak. "Bless you for this."

Dorak looked at Maura with intense longing and pulled her against him. He held her in his gaze for a very long time.

Embarrassed, the new empress looked away. Out of the corner of her eye, she spied a strange woman sitting next to a Bhuttanian nobleman, staring at her with a menacing intensity. Maura recognized the look. It was hate. Hate such as she had never seen in the face of another being.

The woman was an Anqarian with pale skin and yellow hair. She wore expensive but simple clothes of Anqarian design. Something about the pattern in the woman's dress struck Maura as familiar. Her hair was bound by luxurious combs. Judging by her appearance and seating, though Anqarian, she was obviously a person of great importance to the Bhuttanians.

Returning the stare, Maura was surprised to find that the Anqarian did not look away, but continued to scrutinize with great malevolence. The woman's gall unnerved her for just a second. Maura narrowed her eyes at the Anqarian.

The woman's escort, seeing Maura's displeasure, bent his head and whispered into the woman's ear.

Reluctantly, she lowered her eyes.

The man tried to take the woman's hand, but she pulled away.

On the other side of the pale Anqarian sat a little boy. He was about the age of five and had black, curious eyes like Dorak's. The little boy looked at the reigning couple with a blank expression on his face.

It occurred to Maura that the woman may have been

a favorite concubine of Zoar's, and the boy was Dorak's half-brother, perhaps the only one who had survived. It was rumored that all of Dorak's male siblings had met with fatal accidents.

Noticing that his new bride was taken with something, Dorak followed her gaze. Seeing the Anqarian woman, he froze, and his smile was replaced by dark hostility.

The blonde woman, feeling Dorak's eyes, looked pleadingly at him. She put her hand protectively upon the boy's head.

Dorak pulled Maura closer to him.

The woman's face crumpled. Her mouth became pinched and drawn. Leaning her head against the shoulder of her escort, she closed her eyes.

The tall elderly man put his arms around her and leaned his chin against her head. He murmured to her as one does a child. It seemed to soothe her.

Maura turned toward Dorak, but he was no longer concerned with the pale stranger.

He was smiling and waving to the cheering crowd. She was feeling too happy to be concerned at the moment, but Maura would recall the stranger when she was alone.

Dorak led Maura out onto the balcony overlooking the city.

Beneath them stood throngs of people who had come to give their best wishes to the new bride and groom. Already, the story of their queen's coronation was making its way throughout the city.

The only ones unimpressed were the Sivan merchants, who merely shrugged and stated that Dorak could have done no less as it was certainly in his best interest. The Sivans were a practical people.

The Hasan Daegian women banged on drums, children tooted whistles, and the men of households clanged pots.

Prisoners, who had been set free that very hour, were carried through the streets on the shoulders of strangers.

The surviving women from the House of Magi made their way through the crowded streets as best they could. Many of them limped from the effects of torture. Several were so ill they had to wait in the streets until litters could gather them to their new residences that Dorak had established for them.

As they were considered holy women by the Hasan Daegians, no one dared touch their persons. Instead, Hasan Daegian men brought out heaping bowls of soups, platters of bread slathered with melted cheese, and wine. They watched over the starving women as they gobbled the food, making sure no Bhuttanian soldier pestered them.

Hasan Daegian children gave Bhuttanian soldiers on duty flowers. Not knowing what to do with the flowers, but not wishing to offend, they stuck the flowers in between the wedges of their leather chest guards. The children laughed good-naturedly and tried to explain that the flowers were to be worn in their hair.

The soldiers, not speaking Hasan Daegian, merely nodded and continued with their patrols.

The newly-crowned empress laughed also watching the antics of the crowd gathered below the balcony.

Dorak noticed that Maura's crown had become lop-sided and straightened it.

The mere touch of his hand sent a thrill up Maura's spine. All of her senses exploded with color, sound, movement, and touch. She felt as though the nerves in her body had awakened from a deep slumber with every sensation heightened. Her sight and hearing gathered information more quickly than her mind could assimi-late. She felt dizzy and clung to the railing of the balcony festive with flags and garlands of flowers.

"Are you all right?"

"I feel glorious," Maura gushed, shielding her eyes from the midday sun.

"But it is all too much?"

"At times."

"Are you sorry?" asked Dorak, watching her expression intently.

"If our marriage can bring peace, then I am not sorry. You have been most generous today." Maura placed her hand inside Dorak's.

His fingers pressed around hers.

"It is time we see to our guests," Dorak spoke cheerfully.

"Are we not going to the wedding parade?"

Dorak chuckled. "The Lady Sari has seen to all of the arrangements. We are going to have our wedding feast in a pavilion. We shall be able to see all the floats from there."

"And eat, I hope. I am very hungry," said Maura, feeling her stomach growl.

"I see you did not eat breakfast, either. I guess we were both nervous."

Maura nodded enthusiastically in agreement. They waved once more to the cheering crowd and went back into the palace.

Both Hasan Daegian and Bhuttanian guards escorted them to a blue and gold pavilion tent with brightly colored banners hanging from the sides. The tight security inside the pavilion was obvious and gave Maura pause. She realized what a bold thing she had done by marrying Dorak, and as a result, both Bhuttanian and

Hasan Daegian factions hated her.

Dorak was despised as well and had his food tasted by others before he ate. His physician discreetly followed him everywhere with a medical bag full of poison antidotes.

The wedding party made its way to a large platform where tables awaited them.

There stood Sari directing servants and rearranging goblets and silverware. Sari hoped the Bhuttanians would follow Dorak's example and use napkins instead of their sleeves. She also put out the word that she did not want to see meat bones thrown on the ground. Seeing her queen, Sari smoothed her hair before bowing.

"You have outdone yourself, little nanny," Dorak called out so that all could hear. "My bride and I are grateful."

The frown lines on Sari's face softened as she basked in the public praise. She knew she would have little to fear now from any Bhuttanian, as it was clear she was a favorite of Dorak's. There would be no more sulky looks from disgruntled slaves or jostling in the hallways by Bhuttanian soldiers wishing to frighten an old Hasan Daegian woman for pleasure. She would breathe easier.

Maura sat beside her groom. She looked down the

length of their table. The only family representing her was her father's sister, Everlynd, Duchess of Enos, who sat on Maura's left. The rest of the royal family had long since passed on or had been killed during the invasion. For a moment, Maura's happiness was dampened as she became painfully aware of how alone she was in the world.

Her other family, the Dinii, were denied to her. How she wished Empress Gitar and Iegani were present to wish her well. Of course, that was adolescent thinking. Even if they could have come, the proud Dinii, once the Overlords of Kaseri, would have refused to bow to Dorak. And how would she have been able to face Chaun Maaun?

Maura blinked back tears as thoughts of Chaun Maaun raced through her mind. The empress looked around the room quickly, hoping to find something to divert her attention. Her eyes moved across the tent, searching for some juggler or mime that would amuse her. As she scanned the pavilion, Maura again spied the strange woman with the white skin and yellow hair.

She was with the dark-haired little boy with the wide black eyes and the doting elderly Bhuttanian. The woman was seated among those of very high rank in the Bhuttanian party.

Other Bhuttanians came to her table and gave her

the Bhuttanian salute while speaking to her in low tones. Many left small gifts for the boy, which he ignored. He looked sleepy and put his head on the table until his mother gently shook him. He yawned and was given some peeled fruit to eat. The little boy smiled greedily and began to eat the fruit as though ravished with hunger.

The empress turned toward Dorak who was engaged in a philosophical conversation with the High Priest of Bhuttu. Finally getting his attention, Dorak smiled at her. "Husband, who is the Anqarian sitting over there with that Bhuttanian nobleman? She keeps staring at me as though she knows me," spoke Maura. "Should I know her?"

Dorak casually glanced at the table his bride indicated. "The Anqarian way is strange. Pay her no heed."

"I thought everyone not saved by the Dinii had been killed at Anqara or taken as slaves. This woman seems to be important."

Dorak seemed disinterested. "Not everyone," he answered in a husky voice.

"But who is she?"

"A nobleman's wife, nothing more," stated Dorak in a dismissive tone.

"Is she married to that nobleman?"

Dorak was silent for a moment. "No," he said.

"But . . ." Maura continued.

Dorak cut her off. "If the woman bothers you, I will have her removed," he replied, trying to hide his irritation.

"No. I do not wish to cause any reason for discord today," Maura answered dejectedly.

Dorak grunted and returned to his conversation with the High Priest, who was proceeding to make himself drunk on Sivan wine.

Maura looked back and saw the woman with the boy leaving, but not before the Anqarian shot her an undisguised look of loathing as she quit the tent.

The Duchess of Enos leaned close to Maura's ear. "Who is that dreadful woman leaving?"

Maura, not taking her eyes off the retreating Anqarian, whispered, "I do not know, but I'm going to find out."

The Duchess sighed. "Well, I am glad she is going. She's frightful."

Maura nodded in agreement.

At that moment, Dorak leaned over, and in Sivan recited to Maura's aunt a ribald joke that he had just been told by the High Priest.

The duchess, fond of bawdy humor, rolled back her eyes and let out an impolite snort of laughter. She then related the joke to a translator, who whispered it to

Alexanee who was sitting next to her.

The general started to laugh and then stopped short. Frowning, he scolded the duchess in Anqarian, "Women should not know of such things!"

Astonished to find the ruthless general a sexual prude, the duchess turned to the translator, "Tell the honorable Alexanee that he would be surprised at the things I know concerning this subject." She winked seductively at the Bhuttanian.

Flustered, Alexanee sipped his drink, trying to regain his composure.

Later that afternoon and into the evening, a bored Dorak and an enthralled Maura listened to poems and ballads in their honor. The new empress especially liked poems regaling epic deeds, but noticed that Dorak squirmed during the long epics.

Poetry was new to the Bhuttanians, even educated ones like Dorak, but all Bhuttanians loved music. They liked to clap their hands and sing along. Even if they did not know the words, they would make up their own lyrics much to the chagrin of balladeers, trying to perform their compositions.

While listening, Maura ate with relish. Careful not offend anyone, she ate something from both the Bhuttanian and Hasan Daegian dishes presented to her. There were also Sivan and Hittal side dishes. She knew all of the cooks were watching in the wings and anxiously awaiting the opinions of the royal table concerning their elaborate, ethnic dishes.

Dorak ate as well, even handing Maura tidbits on his knife, but only after the food-tasters had consumed from each dish. Under the tablecloth and away from curious eyes, Dorak rubbed his hand over Maura's thigh.

The feel of Dorak's rough hand pleased Maura, and she was glad when it finally came time for the royal couple to excuse themselves for the night. As she walked with her honor guard and a silent Sari trailing behind, Maura could still hear the revelers singing and dancing. The wedding feast would go on for several more days, as was the Hasan Daegian custom. She hoped there would be enough food and patience to go around.

Sari escorted Maura to the bridal suite.

Dorak had the entire set of rooms repainted and new drapes installed.

The Bhuttanians were not much for colors, favoring browns and greys, but Dorak had the walls painted a delicate green. About the rooms were potted ferns and small trees, allowing an outdoor feeling. Soft yellow and pink knickknacks accented the plush emerald furniture.

Maura went from the sitting room to the bedchamber.

A bed with a blue canopy trimmed in gold sat in the middle of the room. The new bride rested on it, sinking into the moss-stuffed comforter and mattress.

Turning, Maura spied her nightgown hanging next to a full-length mirror encased in an exotic wood. It was as Dorak wanted. A simple gown made of common cloth, white and unblemished.

It reminded Maura of a mourning dress except for the blue trim on the bodice. Next to the gown was a robe, carefully folded and made of the same cloth with blue slippers embellished with the uultepes and the Bhuttanian dragon. On closer inspection, Maura could see that the dragon looked as though it was going to bite off the head of one of the uultepes. Maura smirked. Of course, this was Dorak's idea of a joke, or at least she hoped it was.

Across the room was a dressing table holding her toiletries and perfumes. Dorak had thought of everything.

Or perhaps Sari had. As though Lady Sari had overhead Maura's thoughts, she entered tentatively into the room, accompanied by several female noblewomen. "May we help you disrobe?" Lady Sari asked softly. The older woman seemed tired, and her lips were drawn back from her teeth.

Maura noticed she leaned against the doorjamb and

righted herself as an afterthought. "You go to bed at once," Maura scolded. "You need not stay with me. It will be all right."

"But . . ." Sari resisted.

"There is nothing more you can do for me," interrupted Maura, looking intently at her friend and protector. "I must face this alone. You must go now and rest. I will need you in the morning."

Sari's shoulders slumped.

The girl was right.

There was nothing more she could do this night.

Maura must meet with Dorak and face him as best she could.

Sari could not help but fear for Maura but did not let it show on her frazzled face. "As you wish, Great Mother. But if you need anything, you may send for me. I will place a runner outside your door."

Sari's meaning was not lost on Maura. Bhuttanian husbands were known to become violent on the wedding night to assert their dominance.

Although Maura did not believe Dorak would treat her in such a manner, the possibility was unnerving.

It was so un-Hasan Daegian. Hasan Daegian brides and grooms passed their wedding night making love and giving each other gifts that would be treasured throughout their lives together. It was unthinkable to strike a loved one, let alone on such a special night.

The older woman gave the attending women last-minute instructions and exited the chamber, hobbling on her cane.

While the noblewomen attended to her, Maura quietly told one of them to fetch Meagan of Skujpor for Sari.

The woman bowed and slipped out of the room.

The others helped Maura remove her crown. They placed it inside a lockbox. Turning the key, they gave the box to Dorak's man, who retrieved it under guard and left the room.

The noblewomen began undressing the empress, never saying a word due to nervousness on everyone's part. The bridal gown was carefully folded and taken to the laundry room where it would be freshened and then hung on display in the main ceremonial hall.

Hasan Daegian boys of noble birth would file into the hall so they could touch the gown for good luck in hopes of catching a rich and caring wife. It was an honored custom.

Maura studied herself in the mirror. Her eyes seemed too large for her oval face. They had an intense quality that was not pleasing. Brides should have warm and loving eyes, Maura thought. Hers were apprehensive.

The assisting women laid her carefully on a table and

massaged oil into her skin. One brought over a warm cloth to wipe her skin down, but Maura forbade it, thinking of Dorak's wish. The woman seemed surprised but said nothing. Above the reclining empress, the noblewomen glanced at each other.

Relaxed and warm after the gentle and soothing massage, Maura sent the servants away. She donned the nightgown by herself. It felt soft against her skin. Putting on the slippers, she unfolded the robe and put it on as well.

At her night table, the fatigued empress brushed her hair and powdered her face. She looked appraisingly at the haunted reflection staring back at her. "Well, this is the best it is going to get," she remarked.

A knock sounded at the door.

"Enter," called Maura, her heart pounding.

A Bhuttanian slave entered with a tray of finger foods and mulled wine.

Not looking at the empress, the slave put the tray down and kowtowed, waiting for the empress to grant permission to withdraw.

Disappointed that it had not been Dorak, Maura nibbled on a piece of fruit and began humming a tune. Not knowing what to do, she drifted into the sitting room and picked up one of the various manuscripts left on the table.

Startled at the contents, she picked up another. Each one she opened contained love stories with strong erotic overtones. Some even had explicit drawings accompanying them. The love stories were from Hasan Daegian myths, but the drawings were a new element.

Hearing loud footsteps in the hallway, she dropped the drawings and fled into the bedroom, ashamed of herself for being embarrassed. Maura had to smile.

Such sexual material was usually reserved for older married Hasan Daegian women who collected love stories and shared their contents with their younger and shy husbands.

However, was she not the empress of the Bhuttanian Empire? She could read what she wanted.

Maura could not sit still. The stories and their illustrations had inflamed and aroused her.

More footfalls sounded in the hallway. Listening intently, the echoing sounds passed her suite.

Disappointed, Maura sank into the fluffy mattress and listened to the night sounds of the city.

"You are not asleep, are you?" asked Dorak, languishing in the doorway.

Maura jumped. "I did not hear you come in," she said, her words rushing together.

"I know," grinned Dorak.

Maura frowned. She hated the way he kept her off-kilter.

Dorak turned around in full circle. "You like?" he asked, pointing to his outfit. He was wearing a loose-fitting tunic made of the same material as her gown. His long black hair was loose from its usual tight braids and brushed to a lustrous shine. This only added to the allure of his penetrating eyes outlined in kohl. Dorak's feet were encased in simple peasant sandals, but Maura could not help but notice that his toenails sparkled with designs made of gold foil.

Maura looked at Dorak in surprise.

These Hasan Daegian gestures of male beauty were considered decadent for a Bhuttanian warrior.

Behind him, Dorak dragged a little cart laden with beautifully wrapped gifts.

Maura stared stupidly at the gifts.

"I was told the bride and groom exchange gifts on their wedding night. Is this not correct?"

"Yes, yes, it is," stammered Maura, "but I didn't expect you to follow this custom."

Dorak pretended to pout. "Does this mean you have no gifts for me?"

Flustered, Maura began fiddling with the bows on her robe. "I have only one gift."

"Well," said Dorak, looking about the room. "Where is it?"

Maura went to the dressing table and held out a small pouch beautifully embroidered with the uultepes and the Bogazkoy tree.

Dorak stared for a moment at the uultepes entwined around the Bogazkoy. "There is that interesting shrub again. Like the one of which I found the remains in the cave under the palace." Dorak squinted at Maura, whose face became impassive at the mention of the Bogazkoy.

Maura forged a beguiling smile.

Dorak frowned. "You are simpering again," he replied, feeling the weave of the pouch. "Not your style at all."

Chastised, Maura plopped down onto the bed and sank into the moss-filled mattress.

Dorak laughed as he took a running jump and landed down beside her.

For a few seconds, they both bobbed on the soft, springy bed.

Dorak let out a raucous laugh. He gave his new bride a little shove on the shoulder. "Oh, don't be so serious. I'm not going to hurt you," he declared. Dorak winked. "At least, not tonight," he said, his eyes casting a smoldering look at her.

"That is reassuring."

"I should think you are damned lucky that I made you my wife and empress to boot and did not throw you in the dungeon."

"That would be hard as we have no dungeons in Hasan Daeg."

Dorak raised an eyebrow. "An oversight I will have to correct."

Maura grimaced at his suggestion.

"I do not wish to discuss gloomy topics tonight. Being seated next to that boring priest for most of the afternoon was punishment enough. We have the rest of our lives to test our wits against each other, my dear wife. Let us enjoy each other tonight. Tomorrow will bring what it will."

"Agreed," said Maura, somewhat relaxed. She extended her hand and grabbed Dorak around the wrist. "Not enemies tonight."

Dorak grabbed her by the wrist and shook firmly. "Friends tonight and lovers in every sense of the word."

Blushing, Maura withdrew her hand. "Go ahead and open it," she urged, glancing at the pouch.

Dorak pulled open the pouch. He emptied the contents into his hands.

Out fell a ring. It was small but exquisite in workmanship.

Dorak leaned into the lamplight to get a better look at it.

Maura reached over and snatched the ring from

Dorak's palm. She gingerly placed it on each of his fingers until she found one that it fit. "This was the ring my mother gave my father on their betrothal. Do you like it?"

"I am touched that you would give me a gift of such importance to you," replied Dorak, admiring the ring. "What did the ring represent to your parents?"

"The emerald represented my mother and the smaller ruby, my father."

"No," laughed Dorak. "The emerald should have been the man. You Hasan Daegians get everything backwards." He smiled warmly at her. "I am very honored. Thank you."

Maura eyed the wagon full of gifts. "What did you get me?" she asked with childlike glee.

Struggling to climb out of the spongy bed, Dorak was helped by his bride who pushed on his backside. Laughing, he tiptoed over to the wagon and pulled it close. Dorak piled gifts in Maura's lap.

"Which one should I open first?" asked Maura, picking up boxes and shaking them.

"This one," coaxed Dorak, handing her a gaily-wrapped package.

Maura tore open the wrapping and discovered a beautiful sheer negligee inside.

Tiny seed pearls were sewn onto the sheer black

material. "It is wonderful!" exclaimed Maura, holding it up to her torso. "Oh," she said, disappointed. "It makes my skin look too dull."

"Nonsense," said Dorak, gently stroking the material. "It makes you look sensuous."

"Does it, Dorak?" She blinked at the gown. "Somehow, I think this gift is more for you."

"I hope we can both enjoy it." He grinned widely. "Open another one."

Unwrapping a small box, Maura discovered a pair of simple earrings carved out of plain wood.

"These were my mother's," explained Dorak upon seeing Maura's bewildered expression. "This was the only possession she was able to take from her village when she was kidnapped by . . ."

"Your father," Maura finished.

Dorak nodded. "Yes. She wore these nearly every day of her life. One moment, she was a simple girl minding her father's young borax calves in the pasture, and the next, she was wrenched onto a snorting, stampeding horse while watching her village torched. Then she became the Empress of Bhuttan. End of story." Dorak looked saddened by his tale. "I know they do not have the worth of your betrothal ring, but the sentiment is the same."

"Why did she not come to the wedding?"

Dorak smiled bitterly. "She died years ago."

Maura wished to inquire further, but she could see that talking about his mother was difficult for Dorak. She needed him to be in good spirits tonight. Taking out her garnet earrings, she replaced them with the wooden posts. "How do they look?"

"Like they belong to an empress." Dorak smiled, not a mischievous grin or a lecherous glance, but a warm, expressive smile that was without guile.

Maura was overtaken by the masculine beauty that gave Dorak an aura of being strong and true when not posturing.

Dorak took Maura's hand. "I know that we have talked about nothing but our differences. We have argued over policy and debated over political issues. During all this frustrating time, never once did I tire of seeing your face. Never once when you were shouting at me did I wish to be gone out of sight from your angry eyes. I never wanted to send you away."

He stared down at the ring. "It would have been safer and easier for me to banish you or to have you killed." Dorak leaned down and kissed Maura's hand. "But I swear on my mother, I never seriously considered it. I desired you near me as I desire you now." He leaned over and softly kissed his bride on the lips. "Will you have me of your own free will?"

Maura heard herself say, "Yes, I take you of my own free will." Her words inflamed Dorak, and he kissed her more passionately. He stopped abruptly, looking at Maura with wondering eyes.

"Kiss me again, please, Dorak."

Dorak took Maura in his arms. He gently kissed her forehead, cheeks, and throat. Turning her head, he gave baby kisses down the back of her long neck. Encouraged by her soft moans, Dorak continued down Maura's spine, kissing through the fabric of her robe.

Reaching up under the gown, he massaged her buttocks, slowly working his way between her legs.

Maura remained still as her breathing became heavier. She called out his name, her voice raspy.

Able to stand it no longer, Dorak tore the robe and gown off and began caressing Maura's bare skin.

Maura turned toward him, returning his fondling. Roughly, she pulled off his tunic and reached for his manhood, pulling him toward her.

Dorak groaned and followed her commands.

Pleased, Maura pulled Dorak on top of her and began to tease him with the grinding of her hips.

For hours, they made love play, teasing, licking, kissing, and murmuring endearments. Long into the night and early morning, they pleasured each other with touch only.

Finally, Dorak could endure no more and entered Maura.

Maura raked her fingers through his long, dark hair.

Abruptly, Dorak stopped and seemed bewildered.

"What's wrong?" asked Maura, confused at the interruption. "Are you hurt?"

Dorak's face was sour as he put his head down on her shoulder. "No. Let us continue," he answered, his voice vague and troubling.

Realizing Dorak had changed, Maura tried to see into his eyes.

Dorak turned his face away and began moving upon her.

She tried to stop him, but he refused until he gave a strangled cry of release. He collapsed away from her.

Perplexed, Maura reached out to him, but Dorak jerked away. "What is it?" asked Maura in a hurt tone.

"Nothing. Go to sleep," replied Dorak coldly.

Her emotions tangled in a knot, Maura rolled over. Hot, salty tears ran down her face.

Why did Dorak change? All through the night, he had been a caring, considerate lover.

Maura felt his emotions had run deeper than she had anticipated. Then he abruptly changed to a cold, almost hostile partner. Her mind raced over the events of the night. She could think of nothing to cause this reaction.

What had she done?

Exhausted with worry, Maura finally drifted into a restless sleep.

Hearing her rhythmic, ragged breathing, Dorak turned toward her. He touched her damp tresses fanned out on the pillows, thinking of the yellow-haired woman from Anqara and her flaming eyes of hate. Dorak looked at Maura tossing in her troubled sleep and wondered. Would Maura come to hate him as well?

He stroked her cheek lightly, knowing that she would never forgive him for humiliating her so. "You little fool," he said softly. "Why didn't you tell me?"

16

Maura awoke the next morning. Dorak was not beside her.

Swinging her legs over the side of the bed, she groaned. Pulling a rope, the new bride slumped back against the massive wooden headboard carved with the royal crest of the House of de Magela.

The Bhuttanian girl who had nursed Dorak knocked on the bedroom door and entered. She looked around the room sullenly and bowed.

Bhuttanian custom dictated that she should have kowtowed, but Maura chose to ignore the insult. "Please call for Lady Sari," Maura commanded in an even-handed tone. "I wish for a massage."

The slave girl did not cast her soulful eyes to the floor, as was the custom for all Bhuttanian women, but looked directly at the empress. "Sari has been put to bed by the female doctor. She is not allowed to move for several days."

"You may address my nurse as Lady Sari, as is her title. She has a lineage the likes of which your family has never seen, nor will. You are to address me as Great Mother or Empress Maura. If you dare to look at me directly again, especially with those impertinent eyes, I shall slice off a bit of your ear and feed it to you."

The slave scowled at Maura.

They were both the same age, but Maura easily towered over the little nomadic female. Maura knew that even reclining in a bed, she looked imposing.

Still, the girl had courage and spoke her mind. "The Great Aga will not let you touch me!" she spat defiantly.

Maura's fears that this sapling of a girl had been Dorak's bedmate were confirmed, or the little wench would never have dared to speak to her in such a manner. Feeling a spasm of jealousy, Maura swallowed the bile rising from her stomach. "The Great Aga is not always around. Accidents can happen. He would hardly chastise his wife and empress if a slave girl's ear, or worse, got in the way of my dinner knife." Maura let her words sink in. "Think about it, my dear. Make life easy on yourself," said Maura smiling sympathetically at the fuming slave.

The girl, so filled with anger, could not utter a word

and stormed out of the room.

Sighing, Maura donned her robe and went into the hallway where her guards stood.

They snapped to attention as soon as they saw their queen.

Pointing to the young slave muttering as she stomped down the hallway, Maura said, "That girl is never to come close to my person or food again. If she does, kill her."

Several of the female soldiers ran down the hallway and stopped the slave, who protested vehemently. They stored the frightened girl's height, weight, features, and coloring in their memories. As soon as they had burned her image into their minds, they apologized for detaining her.

The girl ran down the hallway, stumbling over jugs and water bags left by the Bhuttanian guards on watch the previous night.

Maura's guards returned and waited for further instructions.

"Inform my servants that I wish to have a bath prepared for me. I want my breakfast tray now."

One of the guards stepped forward. "Perhaps the Great Mother has forgotten that a wedding breakfast has been prepared and is awaiting only the attendance of the bride."

Maura's face went momentarily blank and then took on the expression of one who has received a piece of bad news. "Yes, I had forgotten. Thank you for reminding me," said Maura slowly. "Have my servants attend me. I should make haste. Please relate to Aga Dorak that I have risen and will attend shortly." Maura tried to act nonchalantly. "Where is Aga Dorak?"

"He awaits you in the dining hall, Great Mother. He is talking with guests."

"Of course," Maura responded.

Seeing Bhuttanian soldiers march down the hallway, she hurried inside the apartment and waited for her servants. It wasn't long before her Hasan Daegian attendants scurried into the room to wait upon their newlywed empress.

Being Hasan Daegian, they liked to talk about acts of love but were disappointed when Maura said nothing regarding her wedding night. According to Hasan Daegian custom, the bride would relate anecdotes regarding her husband's prowess in bed. It was considered a sign of respect to boast about one's bedmate.

Hasan Daegian bridegrooms looked forward to hearing the gossip of their mating feats that would follow for weeks after their wedding night.

It was very *Bhuttanian* of Maura to be so reticent and even considered rude.

Although they knew the new empress would have to compromise here and there, the noblewomen hoped she wasn't going native on them.

Maura was soon ready and hurried to the dining hall.

A gong sounded her entrance as she proceeded into the great chamber, looking calm and poised.

With two guards flanking her, Maura acknowledged well wishes and made her way to the royal table. As she did so, she scanned the room for Dorak. Locating him next to her aunt, the Duchess Everlynd, she smiled broadly.

As Maura approached the table, he sprang to meet her and extended his hand to help her into her chair. Maura studied Dorak closely. The anger that she had felt from him last night was nowhere to be found on his handsome face shining in the morning sun. Confused, Maura sat. Seeing Dorak so radiant, Maura could not but suffer that her husband was more handsome than she, causing her to compare herself to a molting Dini chick.

Dorak tapped his goblet with a jewel-encrusted knife that had been brought from his father's tent.

Everyone became quiet.

"You may be seated," Dorak said good-naturedly as he stood next to Maura. "I hope all of you had more of a restful evening than I did."

The Hasan Daegian guests politely twittered as the Bhuttanians remained stone-faced.

The laughter inspired the aga to continue. "I wish to take this time to express my great happiness with this union, both personally and politically. I arose early this morning to compose a song for my bride."

Dorak looked expectantly at Maura. "I did not have time to write any words, but here is the melody. I hope it expresses what I feel." Dorak motioned for the master flutist to approach the royal table.

The flutist wet her lips and raised an oiled-smoothed instrument to her mouth. She began playing a lovely song that was both sweet and sad. The notes turned and twisted in the air, hanging for a few captivating seconds before they floated up to the stained glass windows and out into the busy city.

Maura closed her eyes, thinking of beautiful bubbles shining with iridescent color as they circled shafts of sunlight and then dissipated into the fresh morning air. She opened her eyes only to discover Dorak staring at her with his brilliant eyes seemingly violent in their intensity. Maura quickly looked away. Did she imagine the last disappointing moments of their lovemaking? Perhaps that was the way with Bhuttanian men. *NO! NO! I must trust my instincts,* Maura thought. Dorak had been angry with her. She was sure of it.

Blonde hair swirled before her, and Maura focused on the Anqarian woman who had surfaced in public again. The woman's eyes looked dull as if she was drugged, and her jaw fell slack, giving her mouth a droopy appearance.

Dorak's elderly cousin was with her, but paid little attention, as he seemed enthralled with the music. He noticed the empress looking at their table and gave a friendly smile as he nodded. Then he turned his attention back to the flutist. Finally, the musician finished.

The Hasan Daegians clapped politely while the more enthusiastic Bhuttanians pounded the tables with their hands and whistled.

Realizing that words of appreciation were expected from her, Maura rose. "Good people, it is glad I am that you are present to share my joy. I thank my husband for another wonderful wedding gift. My head is reeling from all that he has bestowed upon me the last several days, especially last night."

Dorak's smile froze on his face.

Maura continued, "But I know that you are hungry, so I will not detain you further by remarking on my husband's amazing attributes, so let's have the morning feast."

Servants brought out trays of freshly baked flatbread, bowls of cooked grain, buns, and morning cakes. Pots of boiled gootee eggs and trays of ripe fruit were so heavy that several women were needed to carry each one out to the awaiting guests.

Jugs of shaybar, the Bhuttanian staple of boiled milk mixed with borax blood, were poured. The Hasan Daegians politely took a sip of the shaybar, quietly gagged, and then returned to their wine and fruit juices.

The breakfast dragged on with the Bhuttanians giving toasts to the couple and singing old Bhuttanian love songs, which sounded like war stories to the more cultivated Hasan Daegians.

As the morning sun drifted into the afternoon sky, Dorak made his excuses for them both and escorted Maura out of the great hall. Once in the back corridor and away from prying eyes, Dorak handed Maura unceremoniously over to Rubank, who had been waiting patiently.

"Where are you going?"

"I have duties to attend," Dorak replied flatly.

"We need to talk,"

"About what, my lady?"

"Last night, our future, everything," retorted Maura, frustrated at Dorak's coldness.

Rubank retreated to a discrete portion of the hallway.

"There is nothing to discuss."

"There is everything to discuss."

Dorak shot her an angry look and, taking her by the elbow, jerked her farther down the hall. "This is not the place nor the time to discuss anything. Nor will I be shouted at by a woman who acts like a fishmonger's wife even if she is the empress."

"How dare you speak to me like that!"

Dorak leaned close to Maura's face. "I shall talk to you any way I like. I am now your husband, and you no longer have rights, but those I grant you."

"That is not true. I am the queen of Hasan Daeg. I have independent rights."

Dorak sneered. "You have nothing, my lady. You should have studied Bhuttanian customs a little closer. You accepted being my empress; therefore, you lost all rights concerning Hasan Daeg. I am now the legal ruler here."

"You bastard!" declared Maura, her fists clenched at her side, ready to strike. Instead, she grabbed his arm, pushing Dorak against the wall with her weight. "That is why the coronation was a surprise!"

"Such tender words from a devoted wife." Dorak motioned to Rubank. "Escort the empress to her chambers and keep her company. I will return this evening to do my husbandly duty."

Rubank looked nervously between Maura and Dorak, not knowing what to do. His face was heavy with confusion.

"You mean to rape me. That's all you Bhuttanians know. Rape. Destruction."

"Are you implying that you were raped last night?" Dorak's face turned crimson, and his lips curled back, giving his face a snarling appearance. "It would be a hard contest to violate you, my lady, when your legs are so readily open."

Maura gasped and struck out.

Dorak caught her hand and encircled her wrist, squeezing mercilessly.

Maura grimaced at the pain, but would not cry out.

Dorak brought all his strength to bear upon Maura. "On your knees before me," he rasped, his voice lined with hate.

The blood rushed from Maura's face and, for a few seconds, her face was as pale as any Anqarian's. The transformation startled Dorak enough to loosen his grip, allowing Maura to break free. Breathlessly, they glared at each other with eyes filled with disappointment and deep pain.

Embarrassed by his lack of control, Dorak pulled his leather gloves from his belt and again waved to Rubank. "Take your mistress to her rooms," he commanded, trying to insert normalcy in his voice.

"How like a Bhuttanian to use a servant to vent his anger upon," sneered Maura. "Do you not see, Rubank, that we both have been ambushed? This is a little game Bhuttanians like to play. If you obey Dorak, then I will kill you because it means you have changed your loyalty. If you disobey, Dorak will have you killed for not following his orders as he is now legally the sovereign of Hasan Daeg, or so that is what he claims. Still, if nothing occurs, your loyalty to me will be in doubt, and I will never trust you again. I will be asking myself why you were waiting in this particular hallway? Why did Dorak single you out to escort me back to my rooms and not my guards? Were you to assassinate me? Put a quiet little knife in the back of my neck?"

Stricken, Rubank lowered his eyes and shook his head, seemingly more from sadness than denial.

Dorak laughed bitterly. "I am not the only one who plays games, eh, my sweet?"

Maura tore her gaze from Rubank's grief-lined face. "I do not know what you mean."

Dorak twisted a twig of Maura's hair between his thumb and index finger. "I think you do, but we will discuss it tonight. I have to go."

Maura pulled away. "Go then. And let the devil take you."

Dorak feigned surprise. "How very Anqarian of you. It must have been the House of Magi's influence upon you."

Before Maura could deny his subtle accusation, Dorak began whistling the composition he had written for her and jaunted down the hallway.

Maura turned her fury upon Rubank, who stood shivering.

Without hesitation, Rubank began undressing and threw his robes, one by one, at Maura's feet.

She picked them up and examined the costly robes carefully, looking for hidden weapons.

Standing naked before her, Rubank lifted his genitals showing his queen that he had not hidden any weapons or poisons and then turned, spreading his buttocks apart.

Satisfied that his anus did not appear swollen or glisten with lubrication, Maura called Rubank over to her.

He knelt before her and opened his mouth. Wrapping the cloth from one of his robes around her finger, she examined Rubank's mouth, looking for pouches or strings tied to one of his molars. All that was in Rubank's mouth were his teeth.

Both of them, stunned at Dorak's treachery and their mutual fear, remained still as though transfigured into stone.

Maura felt Rubank's lips upon her feet, the Hasan Daegian gesture for forgiveness, and jerked away from his touch.

Rubank let out a sound from his tongueless mouth that would cause pity even in the heart of the bravest Bhuttanian warrior. His cry was one of agony and of dreams shattered.

Ashamed, Maura fled Rubank and, upon entering her private chambers, crouched in a corner and cried until the bodice of her dress was drenched with her blue-tinted tears.

Hours later, her servants found her lying on the floor and put Maura to bed.

Meagan of Skujpor was summoned. The healer ran so fast that her cumbersome bosom bounced painfully, but no one laughed as they saw the Magi physician racing toward the empress' private rooms with one hand holding her breasts in place and the other gripping her medical bag.

Even the Bhuttanian guards stepped out of the way for the out-of-breath healer, whom they had grown to respect for saving so many of their own.

Hearing that the empress was ill, Dorak's slave girl ran to Maura's quarters to check for herself. Poking her head inside the bedchamber, she spied Maura looking drawn and pale. Delighted, the girl pranced out of the room and gleefully went about her duties for the rest the day, not aware that a Hasan Daegian guard was shadowing her every move. In the evening, she was found in a laundry basket with her throat slit.

The news of the slave girl's discovery was whispered into Maura's ear. Immediately, Maura's eyes fluttered open, and the empress struggled to sit up. Her throat parched, she greedily drank from a goblet that Meagan held to her lips. Seeing that the empress wished to speak to her in private, Meagan shooed everyone out of the chamber.

"Where is Dorak?" croaked Maura, her voice hoarse.

"He went to visit the army's encampment beyond the city. There are rumors that the Bhuttanians are preparing to move out."

"To where?"

Meagan replied, "I was bandaging the leg of a captain who has gout. He did not realize that I speak Bhuttanian, and I overheard him talking to his next-in-command. He didn't seem to know. He just knew the bulk of the army was going to relocate."

"So Dorak lied to me the entire time."

Meagan lowered her voice. "Maybe not. Perhaps it was this morning's altercation that brought about a change in his mood."

"Does everyone know of our lover's spat?"

"The Bhuttanian girl who nursed Dorak followed you and saw the entire disagreement. She lost no time in telling Bhuttanian servants who then related the story to those Hasan Daegians who understood Anqarian. Of course, we don't know for sure what she related was true, but the fact you were rolling on the floor again would indicate some of what she was spreading might be true."

"I am glad the little bitch is dead."

Meagan merely shrugged. "I certainly won't lose any sleep over her absence. She never changed Dorak's bandages properly. It so irritated me that she would not follow my instructions."

"Poor Rubank. Dorak and I have disgraced him."

"Rubank is a servant of the Royal House of de Magela. He is used to sacrificing."

Maura interjected, "Will he ever forgive me?"

"Forgiveness may not be coming for a very long time, but what choice did you have? You can trust no one. You are now the wife of the Bhuttanian Aga, the most powerful and hated man in the world. A lot of people want to see you dead. And if you die, what will happen to the Hasan Daegians? There is no offspring to take your place. You are the last of the de Magelas. You must survive! It is imperative!"

"Trust no one. Not even you, Meagan of Skujpor?"

Meagan returned Maura's sad gaze. "No one," she mouthed silently. After a short pause, she turned to the business, which was foremost on her mind. "Why do you go into a sort of coma every time you have an altercation with Dorak? These trances must stop. You must be able to rouse yourself quickly after a stressful episode with this man. These fits put you in danger."

"I do not think they have anything to do with Dorak. He may only be a conductor."

"What do you mean?" asked Meagan who forgetting protocol, as usual, sat on the edge of the bed.

"I do not put myself in these trances. I feel compelled to slip into the dream world. I am convinced the Black Cacodemon is on the palace premises somewhere so that he can be close to me. I think he acts through Dorak without Dorak's knowledge. As I said, Dorak acts as a conductor. The wizard feeds upon my fear. He uses my own emotions against me."

"The palace has been searched. The Black Cacodemon is not inside the premises. No one has seen him since the fall of O Konya."

"Sari thought she heard him laughing in the court-yard after the duel."

Meagan looked at Maura doubtfully.

"I am telling you that he is somewhere on the palace

grounds." Maura struggled to get out of bed and fell back against the headboard. Rubbing the sides of her temples, she tried to clear her head of the fog that seemed to impede her thinking. "What time is it?"

Meagan rubbed the empress' body with a soothing lotion. "It is after dark."

"Dorak will expect me to be in the bridal chamber."

"You are still going to meet Dorak after this morning?" asked Meagan, alarmed.

"I cannot give him an excuse to imprison me. I must not let him see me defeated. Help me please."

Meagan gave Maura a stimulant, which would help her to move without sluggishness. With Meagan's help, she dressed and combed her tangled hair. Squaring her shoulders, the determined empress entered the hallway and, moving in step with her guards, returned to the bridal suite where she knew Dorak would come for her sooner or later.

The empress waited in the chamber.

For two days, Dorak did not appear. On the third day, Dorak returned. He sauntered into the bedroom with an air of jocularity until he spied the wagon full of gifts still unopened. "You have not opened these," he said.

Maura gave him a look of disgust. "As if they mean anything."

"If they do not, it is because of your treachery!" Dorak cried. He seemed on the edge of losing control as he paced about the room.

Maura studied him.

His face was unshaven, and his clothes were stained with dollops of food.

"I don't understand you, Dorak. One moment, you seem calm and at peace. The next, you are babbling nonsense." Maura went over to him by the window and gently touched his shoulder. "I thought our night together was special. We were like a real husband and wife. You were so gentle and caring that I thought . . ."

Dorak interrupted, "You thought what?"

Maura took note of the warning in Dorak's voice. "That perhaps we could care for one another, but you turned on me. I know not what for. You hurt me. Look!" Maura rolled back the sleeve of her gown and showed the bruises, which colored her arm.

Dorak winced when he saw the bruises and turned away, looking upon the city. "I am sorry that I hurt you. I was angry."

"But why?" asked Maura, who could feel the beginning of tears in the making.

"You were not a virgin!" cried Dorak, slamming himself against the wall. He sank down to the floor and put his head into his rough-looking hands. "By Bhuttanian custom, I should have you executed."

Maura stood rooted to the floor, stunned.

Dorak moaned and pounded his leg with his fist.

Maura came out of her stupor and grabbed Dorak's hand, placing it between her breasts.

Dorak let out a small sob.

"I do not understand, Dorak. Please help me."

Dorak lifted his face. There was no malice or cunning stalking the lines of his face, only pain. "Bhuttanian law requires virgin females for all husbands, especially the royalty. Any woman found not to be chaste is stoned to death by her husband's relatives. This is how we ensure the bloodline through the male."

"I am not Bhuttanian." Maura sank beside Dorak and leaned against his shoulder. "I never told you that I was a virgin. You never asked me."

"You were the only daughter of the ruling queen. I assumed you were unspoiled."

"Dorak," said Maura, trying to keep her voice even. "Ruling queens don't marry until after the age of three hundred. Did you expect that there would be three hundred-year-old virgins?" Maura started to laugh. "I mean, just think of it, who could stand living like that? Besides, we expect the males to be virgins . . . not the females." Maura threw back her head and let the laughter escape unchecked.

Dorak shook her angrily. "This is not a game. You could lose your life over this."

Maura could not stop laughing. She felt hysterical. "I am not killed for trying to destroy you. I am not killed in battle. I am not killed because I am queen. I am not killed because I pose a threat to your throne. My death will be because I had sex before I met you." Maura broke out in new peals of laughter. "Oh, this is too much. I mean, I don't know what stoning is, but I imagine that it has to do with rocks that are used in a most unpleasant way. Ha, Ha, Ha!"

Dorak held Maura close and rocked her like a small child. Laying her head against his chest, she was comforted by the musky, outdoor smell that always accompanied him.

"If you are going to kill me, then let me at least die as a warrior. Let me end my life with honor." She hiccupped. "This custom of yours is most cruel and barbaric. To demand of women that they not make love until they wed is hideous. Most hideous."

"It has been the way of our people for centuries." Dorak kissed the top of her head.

Maura felt his warm breath on her skin.

"Who knows of this lover?" asked Dorak.

"I do not know who knew. We were trying to keep it a secret until after the war."

"That is good that it was hidden. Tell me your lover's name."

Maura stiffened in Dorak's arms. "If I tell you, then it would not be a secret any longer."

"You would protect this man even if it means your life?" asked Dorak incredulously.

Maura pushed her way out of Dorak's arms and faced him. "You have no intention of killing the queen of Hasan Daeg. Without me, there would be total insurrection. You need me, and we both know it. You want to know his name for your own reasons, to hurt someone I love. I will not let you hurt anyone that I love ever again!"

Dorak pulled Maura to her feet and threw her across the room. She landed with a dull thud. Defiant, she continued, "I am Hasan Daegian. Your laws did not apply to me until after you conquered my territory. If you kill me, it will be seen as murder, but you don't care about any of that. You are just crazy with jealousy!"

"Was it Chaun Maaun? Was it?" Enraged, Dorak fell upon Maura and pounded his fists upon her chest and stomach.

Pinned down by Dorak's weight, she reached behind her and felt for an object. Picking up something heavy from the floor, Maura swung and hit Dorak in the forehead.

The blow stunned him long enough for Maura to lift her leg and kick Dorak hard in the stomach.

Grunting, Dorak fell back with a loud thump.

Knowing she could not risk seriously harming Dorak, Maura scrambled for the door only to have Dorak tackle her. Maura flipped on her back so she could have her hands free to block his punches.

"You crazy spawn of a bastard. You show your true colors at last! You are insane!" Maura cried out. Tasting blood in her mouth, she spat in Dorak's face, infuriating him more.

He grabbed her hair and began banging her head against the floor.

Believing that Dorak was angry enough to kill her, Maura could hear her guards pounding on the door. She had to stay alive until they could get into the locked room. She wrapped her powerful legs around Dorak's waist and flipped him over as she grabbed onto his nose and gave it an awful twist.

His nose ring ripped through the fleshy part of his nostril. Dorak howled with pain. His hands flew up to cradle his bleeding face.

Losing no time, Maura hit him in the neck to disable him, but the blow was not strong enough to put him under.

Reeling from Dorak's pummeling, Maura crawled

away from him and pulled herself up on a divan. Out of the corner of her eye, she saw Dorak make for her again. She swung around and kicked him in the groin as hard as she could.

Dorak stumbled but still came at her. There was murder in his eyes.

Maura had never felt so terrified, even in battle.

Battle was impersonal, but Dorak wanted to kill her, his wife, in a blind rage over what she considered a trifle.

Maura flung herself at the door and twisted the knob in desperate hope. It would not turn. She was trapped. Turning, she faced Dorak as he stalked her. His face was dark and menacing, wild with confusion. "Dorak, please don't," Maura pleaded. "You do not know what you are doing. If you kill me, the entire city will rise. O Konya will be as Anqara, and all of your work will be for naught."

Dorak halted at the sound of her terrified voice. His face became unclouded as his black eyes focused on her swelling and bloody face. His face felt wet as he wiped his hand across it. It was smeared with red blood . . . his blood. Dorak's mouth fell open in disbelief. He stepped back from her. "What am I doing?" Dorak gasped.

The Hasan Daegian guards burst into the room through the balcony on ropes tied from the rooftop.

Seeing their queen flattened against the door, they ran to her, throwing furniture out of the way. More Hasan Daegian guards dropped onto the balcony and quickly surrounded Dorak. One of the guards took out a dagger hidden in her boot and started to approach Dorak.

"NO!" cried Maura as she blocked the guard's arm. "Leave him be. Just get me out of here. Take me to Lady Sari."

The largest of the guards picked Maura up in her arms and carried her away.

Hearing Bhuttanian boots rushing on the stone floor, the guards ran the other way toward Sari's quarters.

Watching them flee, Dorak slumped against the door jamb, bellowing, "MAURA, DON'T LEAVE ME!"

17

Sari's apartment was not spacious.

Still, it was of adequate size and comfortable with plush furniture. A young girl of eight opened the door as the guards rushed in carrying the queen. The little girl's eyes widened, and she hurried to Sari's bedside crying, "Oh, my lady, the empress is here to see you! She looks as though she has had a fall!"

Sari had been resting comfortably in her bed when she heard the commotion in the next room. She rose quickly and put on her robe with the little girl's help. With the aid of a cane and the girl, Sari hobbled into her sitting room. The old woman clutched at the collar of her robe when she saw the queen, battered and beaten, sitting in one of her rocking chairs. "What happened?"

Maura dismissed her bruises and cuts with a wave of her hand and bade Sari to sit.

The Hasan Daegian guards faced the door, ready for anything amiss. They would not fail their mistress as they had in the sacred grove of her ancestors.

The little girl gave several of them a start when she came up behind them and began fondling their clothes and armor, her mouth opened in amazement.

"Nani, get away from those women. You bother them," Sari scolded.

Nani returned a mischievous grin that showed her missing several of her front teeth.

One of the guards smiled back at her, but only for an instant.

The little girl skipped over to Sari's chair, where she casually plopped down at the woman's feet.

"Who is this?" Maura asked.

"This is my adoptive daughter, Nani, who will take Mikkotto's place as head of the family as my grandchildren have been disinherited. Nani is a distant kinswoman and has Sumsumitoyo blood."

Maura hid her surprise that Sari had spoken Mikkotto's name.

Sari, who had abdicated her position as matriarch of her family to serve the de Magelas, had not spoken her granddaughter's name to anyone since Mikkotto had thrown down the family's ancestral fan in the Council of Elders and Nobles.

Maura grunted her approval in Bhuttanian fashion and paid the girl scant attention.

"Dorak do this?"

"If you think I look bad, you should see him," replied Maura, trying to sound jovial.

"This attack," asked Sari, putting her words together carefully, "was unprovoked?"

"He hit me first if that is what you are asking."

"Then perhaps nothing more will come of it. It was just another Bhuttanian husband chastising his wife."

"This was a beating," corrected Maura, touching her left eye, which had swollen shut. "Dorak has had opportunity to use force with me before, but he has always chosen the quieter path. This is a rash act, even for him."

Sari thoughtfully folded her hands in her lap as she considered the situation. "Perhaps now that he is your husband, he thinks he may do as he pleases."

"I think he intends to kill me."

"For what purpose?" inquired Sari, not believing Maura's theory. "With you, he has everything. Without you, he will struggle to hang on even with the help of the Black Cacodemon."

Maura leaned forward in her chair. The hair stood on her arms, and the moist air suddenly seemed chilled. "You did not see his eyes, Sari. He was truly mad."

Sari unfolded her smoking pouch, offering some to her queen.

Maura made a cheroot from the herbs and various papers presented for her selection.

Sari made herself one, which Nani gaily lit.

While considering her predicament, Maura watched the smoke drift toward the wooden beams that supported the ceiling. She waited for Sari to speak.

"I am not a wise woman like those from the House of Magi, but I have lived for many years. Dorak's actions are not what they appear." Sari drew on her cheroot. "Perhaps there is another explanation."

"What do you mean?"

"I have discovered the identity of the blonde Anqarian woman." She paused for effect.

"Well?"

Sari settled back in her chair. "The woman is Princess Jezra. She is one of the few survivors from Anqara before the siege started. Her father was one of the most distinguished bankers until he fell in disgrace."

"Why is that?"

"He is said to have left Anqara with his family and all his belongings several weeks before Zoar showed up at the city gates."

"Could be a coincidence."

"I hardly think so with the man's daughter appearing

ABIGAIL KEAM

at the marriage ceremony. Many say that her father loaned much of the his wealth to Zoar to finance wars, and with this, he bought the safety of himself and his family. Jezra was his only child and is rumored to be like her deceased father, intelligent and ruthless."

"But why would that cause her to look at me with such hate?"

Sari was very tired by all the palace intrigue. "Little sparrow. Dorak has addled your brain. I said she was called Princess Jezra. Anqara has no royal family. The city was ruled by a democratic council with a mayor at the head. One is only a princess by birth or by marriage to a prince."

Maura realized the implications of Sari's words, and the knowledge screamed through her mind like a howling banshee. "She is Dorak's wife!"

"Yes," said Sari sympathetically. "And the child with the dark river eyes is Dorak's firstborn. He is the child Jezra wishes to see ascend to the throne of Bhuttan. Make no mistake, she is your dangerous opponent, and she is not bound by the honor code of a warrior."

Leaning back in her chair rocking, Maura inhaled deeply the sweet smoke of her cheroot. "I don't feel my heart anymore."

"It's a shock, I know."

"You think Jezra put Dorak up to this?"

"No," Sari said emphatically. "I think it is a possibility she may have slipped something in Dorak's wine to make him aggressive, but I do not think she has any influence over him. He did not seem pleased to see her at the wedding."

"Whatever the reason, I must be away from here," said Maura, her voice sounding odd.

"You must go to the Mother Bogazkoy."

"Yes, you are right," the empress murmured, gazing at her hands as if in a drunken stupor. Her mind reeled from the day's events. Images of Iegani and Gitar whistled through her mind. She saw Yeti taking her out flying over the high cliffs and then dropping her thousands of feet with only a nervous Tarsus to catch her as she fell through the clouds. That was to make her tough and trust the Dinii as she trusted nothing else. She saw her mother observing tutors as they worked with her, and her father teaching her to lace her sandals. So many people had spent countless hours teaching her to become a noble warrior, an astute politician, and a worthy queen. How had she repaid those who had been selfless with their time and knowledge? How many had sacrificed their lives for her? There were her parents and many more. Maura felt a deep and unrelenting shame.

"Sari, will you help me?"

"Yes, little sparrow," said Sari, observing the changes upon Maura's face.

"Even if it means great peril or the supreme sacrifice?"

Sari paused for a moment. Her face became mottled with emotion. "I live only to serve the House of de Magela."

18

Dorak put the torch out.

"You have come."

"Yes," was all Dorak could reply.

The Black Cacodemon moved about the small windowless chamber. Dust floated beneath his black robe and drifted about the hem. "And she thinks you are mad and going to kill her?"

"Yes."

"If not you, then your harpy of a first wife. By now, word of her identity should have spread throughout the entire palace." The wizard chuckled under his foul breath.

Dorak could smell it from where he stood.

"It was brilliant to bring that woman to the wedding. I am surprised that Jezra did not scratch the Hasan Daegian bitch's eyes out the moment she saw her." The

Black Cacodemon's shoulders fell as though disappoint-ed that she hadn't. "And the whining that you didn't mean to hit her was a masterful touch."

Dorak said nothing, staring belligerently at the eerie being in the black robe. He could see very little of the wizard's features. Just a sliver of cheekbone, a knotted finger pointed in the darkness, and a glimpse of pale, thin lips. Dorak restrained from shuddering.

"You have regrets?" asked the Black Cacodemon softly, his face covered by the black cowl of his robe.

Again, Dorak was silent.

"Ah," replied the Black Cacodemon. "I sense the truth unspoken in this room. You have feelings for this girl."

"She is not to be harmed," spoke Dorak forcefully, his dark eyebrows arching.

The Black Cacodemon hissed a long drawn out breath. Droplets of moisture were illuminated by a shaft of moonbeam that fell through a crack in the mortar. "I cannot guarantee this. If General Alexanee finds out that she is not a virgin, he will have no recourse but to kill her."

"The only way he will know that is if you tell him. He is going back to Kittum soon, so I don't see that as a problem, do you?"

"Still, it was a good reason to put her on guard. Let

us hope she runs tonight."

"If she does, all we will do is follow."

The Black Cacodemon made a conciliatory gesture with his hand. "Of course, we can restrain ourselves until she reaches the Mother Bogazkoy, but then she must be stopped. She must never touch the flesh of the Bogazkoy. How she is stopped is up to you, Great Aga. It may call for an arrow through the heart." The wizard circled Dorak and whispered in his ear. "Are you up to it?"

Dorak leaned away from the odious being who made his skin crawl.

The Black Cacodemon became still. "Shh, can you hear it? She is healing herself. Hear the buzz?" The black-robed man raised his head and sniffed the air. "She is healing the old one as well." He raised his hands in the night air. "Minor ailments, but it will sap her energy and slow her down."

It was Dorak's turn to laugh. "I have yet to see that."

The wizard, not liking to be mocked, spoke sharply, "This would all be unnecessary if the code from the tattoo had been broken."

"The design does not match any description found in writings from the House of Magi. I think Abisola had the royal tattoo altered to confuse us. She knew we would locate the secret in ancient manuscripts sooner or later."

The wizard inhaled the dark, moldy air deeply. "A worthy woman she was, but her triumph was small and will not last. In the end, we will learn the secret of the Bogazkoy, and its power to grant immortal life." He ran his hand along the damp walls, his long ragged nails scraping against the stone. "What of Mehmet's journals?"

"Nothing," lied Dorak, his face throbbing where Maura had hit him.

The Black Cacodemon chuckled. "She was worthless as an informant. All those years on your father's payroll, and he didn't even know she had taken a Dini as her lover. What makes the story amusing is that she spent years secretly helping your father's opponent." The wizard snorted. "Your father had such a way with women. No doubt he bedded Mehmet roughly in his youth, and she turned on him because of it. She was originally from Bhuttan, was she not?" He spread out his hands. "It would only make cosmic justice."

Dorak, not wishing to hear of his father's lovers, changed the subject. "I'm positive Maura thinks the Mother Bogazkoy will infuse her with the same power the offspring gave to Abisola. Nothing more."

"That is good. It would not do for her to realize its

true potential. She would fight like a demon to gain this power."

Through the gloom, Dorak thought he could see something that might have resembled a smile, but looked like an angry slash that revealed dirty, chipped teeth. "What will happen if she does reach the Mother Bogazkoy first?"

The Black Cacodemon's head tilted toward Dorak. "We shall have to kill her immediately and drink her blood as it flows from her veins. The effect on us will not be as potent, but it could extend our lives by five hundred years, give or take."

Dorak pressed against the wall. "I will not do that!"

"Dorak, I am surprised. You have killed before. You even murdered your father while he was taking a piss."

"How do you know that?" Dorak hated this room and the stench that reeked from its walls.

"Dorak. Dorak. I know everything." The Black Cacodemon raised his cowled head and peals of laughter rippled from his throat. The cowl fell backwards exposing the wizard's misshapen, scarred head.

Dorak shrank back against the wall. He turned and blindly felt for the door. His clumsiness only encouraged the Black Cacodemon to laugh harder—high-pitched squeals combined with snorts that sounded like an animal being strangled. Dorak discovered the door lever and wrenched the door open.

As he ran down the hallway, he heard the wizard call after him, "Next time, don't be so long between visits! I do so love our little chats."

19

A drunken Bhuttanian was enticed.

He followed a half-dressed Hasan Daegian guard calling to him sweetly into a horse stall. Several minutes later, the guard emerged with the dead Bhuttanian's clothing.

Other Hasan Daegian guards stepped out of the darkness and buried the Bhuttanian under a mound of straw. In the warhorses' drinking buckets, they mixed a golden liquid with water, causing the horses to slumber. Finished with their macabre business, the guards left as quietly as they had come and melted into the darkness.

An hour or so later, the empress, wearing a hooded cloak stepped from Sari's room and, with her guards, began stealthily negotiating the palace hallways.

The Hasan Daegian women unsheathed swords that had been stolen from the armory and quickly dispatched any Bhuttanian soldier on duty with cunning and speed. The group made their way down hallway after hallway to the first floor of the palace, leaving a legacy of bloody carnage behind. Before them stretched the expansive courtyard and the garden.

If they could make it to the end of the garden, they would escape through a hidden door the Bhuttanians knew nothing about and melt into the city.

Cries of alarm sounded in the palace.

The Hasan Daegians realized they had been discovered. They bolted for their lives through the courtyard just ahead of advancing Bhuttanian soldiers.

The empress, in her hooded cape, stumbled and fell to her knees.

Two guards immediately pulled her up and began running with her. One of the guards took an arrow through the heart and fell. Another guard immediately took her place at the side of the empress.

Several guards took the rear, acting as shields knowing they would be cut down any second as they ran over the rough cobblestones of the courtyard.

The stones were slick from rain, reducing the Hasan Daegians' speed as they strained to reach the secret door.

Only the empress knew of its precise location, and if luck prevailed, they needed only a few more minutes.

Without warning, Bhuttanian soldiers, roused from their sleep, rushed at them from the left.

The Hasan Daegian women surrounded their queen and faced the oncoming enemy. They fought valiantly but could make no headway toward the secret door. One by one, the combatants fell until both Hasan Daegians and Bhuttanians were strewn about the courtyard like broken toys.

Alexanee, dressed in his nightshirt, pushed his way to the front and held up his hand.

The exhausted Bhuttanian soldiers pulled up their swords.

"Will you surrender?" he cried.

The hooded queen spoke nothing but shook her head vehemently.

The Bhuttanian Commander ordered his men to move away from the small knot of women and their quivering queen. He sent a runner to find Dorak. "Great Mother, I cannot permit you to leave. Please, please do not commit this folly," he begged. His hand was firm upon his sword as he looked over his shoulder to see if the aga was coming.

The hooded empress began inching her way toward the courtyard wall.

Bhuttanian soldiers moved to intercept but made no attempt to strike at the women.

At once, the general had a brilliant idea. He laid down his sword and ordered the rest of his men to do so.

The Bhuttanian soldiers reluctantly followed suit.

The general displayed his open hands as he slowly moved toward his new empress. "Great Mother," he said to the dark-clad woman. "Have mercy on me. Do not make me the only Bhuttanian in history to strike down his ruling lady."

The Bhuttanian empress remained motionless inside the tiny knot of Hasan Daegian guards.

"HALT!" a voice boomed from the darkness. Dorak swept out of the blackness and into the timid light of handheld torches. "Maura, stop this! You are surrounded and cannot escape. Think of your women." He seemed more irritated than angry.

The empress did not move.

After several minutes, Dorak grew impatient. "Either surrender at once, or I will cut your guards down."

Again, the cloaked empress did not move.

Dorak turned to Alexanee, "Kill them, but leave my wife untouched."

The Hasan Daegian guards moved into a closer knot around their queen.

Alexanee picked up his sword, as did the others.

They outnumbered the Hasan Daegians four to one.

The Bhuttanian soldiers scowled as they waited for the order to attack. They couldn't help but think this was outright butchery. And what if one of them slipped on the wet cobblestones and struck the empress instead?

General Alexanee raised his hand and looked beseechingly at Dorak one last time.

Dorak stared straight at the cloaked empress, who did not return his gaze.

With a final sigh, Alexanee lowered his hand. The Bhuttanians rushed the little group of women.

The women did not flinch but waited as the silent men overcame them. As they struck swords with the Bhuttanians, they cried out, "FREEDOM FOREVER!"

The men made quick work of the remaining Hasan Daegian guards, causing their deaths to be as painless as possible. The Hasan Daegians looked at their killers gratefully before closing their eyes one last time.

The soldiers, wiping blood from their swords before sheathing them, looked at their general with wide, questioning eyes.

Alexanee, understanding the unspoken request, nodded.

Four Bhuttanians stood with each slain Hasan Daegian guard. With a solemnity reserved for one of their own, the Bhuttanian soldiers picked up each Hasan

Daegian woman. Two holding the legs and two more raising the body under the shoulders, the Bhuttanians slowly marched the bodies over to where a crowd of Hasan Daegians from the palace stood watching the sad spectacle. The soldiers turned the bodies over to the Hasan Daegian servants and stood with the bereaved group as Dorak faced the defiant and silent empress.

Dorak was beside himself with fury. He was not sure if it was because Maura had placed herself in such a dangerous situation or that her attempt to escape had failed. "There is nowhere to go," Dorak said, his voice swollen with anger. He started toward Maura.

The empress flinched and stepped back.

Dorak ran and caught the flailing woman in a bear hug. He felt like crushing her in his powerful arms. Dorak began squeezing Maura.

She gasped out loud.

Dorak let go. Something was wrong.

The woman felt too soft.

Fearing he had been duped, Dorak pulled back the cloak's hood.

Staring back at him with huge, fearful eyes was not Maura.

"Sari!" cried out Dorak. He violently shook the old woman. "Where is she? Tell me or I will torture you until you don't even know your own name," he threatened.

Sari struggled with Dorak. Pushing him back, she stumbled to the ground. Her hand came upon a short sword. "I'll tell you nothing, you bastard!" she cried as she fell upon the sword.

Dorak rushed to stop her but felt her warm blood rush upon his hands as he reached for her. Pulling the sword out, he tried to staunch the bleeding. "Sari, no! Sari!" he kept calling, but the old woman was already dead.

20

Meagan was binding wounds.

The Hasan Daegian guards had killed over fourteen Bhuttanian combat soldiers and wounded fifteen before they entered the courtyard.

Tears flowed down her face as she tended to the living. She was both horrified at the savagery of the Hasan Daegian attack yet proud of the damage they had inflicted.

Many Bhuttanians had been mutilated upon the face and genitals. Some had been castrated.

Meagan barked, "What is this?"

Her assistant lurched as though she would vomit.

A soldier had been brought in with his face cut into ribbons with bits of bone exposed. This made the third Bhuttanian soldier whose face the Hasan Daegian women sliced away.

Meagan felt for a pulse.

There was a faint one.

She looked at her initiate. "Compose yourself. I need caromate," she said without rebuke.

The initiate took dry herbs out of the medical bag and placed them in a clean cloth. Taking the cloth between her hands, she ground the fabric to break the herbs inside. Taking a short whiff, she nodded to Meagan and placed the cloth over what remained of the mouth and nose of the soldier. He struggled for a few seconds and fell into a deep sleep.

Meagan took a blue liquid from her bag and put a few drops on the soldier's tongue. He fell into a painless death. "May Mekonia have mercy on your soul," Meagan said.

"And ours," echoed the young initiate.

Meagan moved over to the next soldier who also had a bloody mask for a face. "It looks like they started on this one but didn't finish," remarked Meagan as she took a cloth with ointment to wipe the blood off.

The soldier's hand reached up suddenly and grabbed Meagan's hand in a vise grip.

"What's this?" exclaimed Meagan, feeling alarmed.

The grip on her hand tightened.

Meagan peered closer.

The skin of the soldier had tints of blue.

Meagan reached over to her bag and pulled out a surgeon's knife.

Holding on to the soldier's hand, she pricked a finger.

A tiny drop of blue blood oozed from the small nick.

Meagan immediately wiped the droplet from sight and put a bandage on the finger.

"Help one of the others," said Meagan to her initiate. "I don't need you with this one."

"But . . ." argued the initiate.

"His vitals are stable. I'm just going to put him to sleep and attend the worst ones until I can get back to him," she said, breaking some herbs under the soldier's nose.

"But it looks as though he has been castrated," persisted the woman.

Meagan gave the novice a stern look.

The initiate wandered over to another table where the flesh from a sword wound was being sewn together.

Dorak, following soldiers carrying the body of Sari, staggered in.

Sari was placed neatly in a row of the dead awaiting funeral preparations.

Dorak stared numbly at the row of dead Bhuttanian soldiers, Hasan Daegian guards, and Sari. He seemed bewildered.

For a moment, Meagan almost pitied him. She leaned down to the ear of the soldier in her care and whispered, "Dorak is here. Move not if you care for your life."

An officer addressed Dorak, which caused him to come out of his stupor.

The officer was ordered to search high and low for the empress. Every room in the palace was to be searched as was every house in O Konya. The officer pressed his fist against his chest and hurried off.

Seeing Meagan, Dorak stormed over. "I don't suppose you would know where your empress is?" he asked Meagan sarcastically.

"I'm sure the empress will turn up, most likely under our noses, Great Aga."

"What is wrong with him?" asked Dorak, pointing to the soldier whose face was swollen and black-blue from massive facial cuts.

Meagan was suddenly very afraid. She looked timidly at her feet. If Dorak knew, he would strike them all dead.

"Well, speak up," demanded Dorak, his patience wearing thin.

"Some of the soldiers had their faces disfigured, and some were castrated." She pointed to the groaning soldier. "This one they started but didn't finish."

Dorak seemed taken back. "Is it customary for Ha-san Daegians to disfigure their enemies?"

"No, Great Aga."

"By the eyes of Bhuttu, I thought Sari was enough, but this . . . " Dorak waved to the dying men in Mea-gan's care. "This is most vicious."

"Great Aga, these men must be removed to the hospital in O Konya. There simply is not enough room or medical supplies to care for them properly in the palace."

"Take them to the infirmary near the barracks."

"Your soldiers have taken over the infirmary for living quarters. These wounded men need help quickly."

"Fine, fine," answered Dorak impatiently. "Move these men where you will. Supply them anything they need."

"Yes, Great Aga. I will move the men immediately to the hospital," replied Meagan relieved. She snapped her fingers at the waiting servants and Bhuttanian slaves who would carry the wounded to wagons and on to the city hospital.

Her assistants gathered their instruments and walked alongside the stretchers, comforting the wounded while pushing the Bhuttanian physicians out of their way. Hasan Daegian medicine had been deemed superior to the Bhuttanian way. Even Dorak did not interfere with the Hasan Daegian healers, giving them free reign.

This caused many of the Bhuttanian physicians, who were little more than temple priests, to protest vehemently. However, the wiser of the Bhuttanians, who tired of their patients dying from infection and blood loss, began studying the techniques and philosophy of Hasan Daegian medicine.

Meagan had grown weary of these meddlesome old men who peered constantly over her shoulder and dirtied her clean instruments with their unwashed hands. She knew that one of the reasons she was not in prison was due to teaching Bhuttanians things as simple as washing one's hands before touching a patient.

The death rate of Bhuttanian infants had gone down drastically under her supervision. Meagan could not help but think she was contributing to the demise of her people by helping the Bhuttanians.

Now before her lay the Hasan Daegian queen disguised as a Bhuttanian warrior with a badly wounded face. Meagan was going to get her off the palace grounds and into the city, even if it meant her death. This act was going to be her redemption. Meagan breathed easily as she felt the weight of guilt lift from her shoulders. She even began enjoying herself as she followed Maura's stretcher outside and loaded it onto the wagon carrying other patients. So, as not to call undue attention to the queen, Meagan tended to other soldiers in the wagon.

The driver made short work of the trip to the hospital, located in the middle of O Konya. Built a century before, it was one of the tallest buildings in the garden city. The first floor housed the sick and injured, and the second and third were used for lodgings and research.

The women from the House of Magi had taken over the top floor when they had come as refugees to O Konya and lived there still—what remained of them.

As Hasan Daegians rarely got sick, the lower floor was used to treat injuries from accidents. Much of the time, it had been empty until the war came.

Now it was always busy with Bhuttanians due to this and that. Much of the illness was caused by the lack of hygiene. Simple cuts became infections, colds turned into pneumonia, and rotten teeth became poisonous to the entire body. The most common medical problem suffered by the Bhuttanians was blindness caused by the lack of certain nutrients in their diet.

But Meagan pushed all of these worries from her mind as she jumped out of the wagon, shouting orders concerning her patients. She waited by the main entrance until all of the patients were unloaded and taken inside.

Then she ordered patients to specific rooms, putting the empress in a room with a dying Bhuttanian—a boy really.

Meagan placed the queen over by the window and leaned over. "The boy is unconscious. He can hear and see nothing. He will die very soon."

The woman on the table did not respond to Meagan's reassurances but moaned like a soldier in great pain.

Meagan pressed her hand against the shoulder of the disguised woman, saying, "May Mekonia be with you," and left the room.

An hour later, she came back with her white gown covered in blood and her face dirty.

The young boy was dead as Meagan expected he would be.

The bed by the window was empty.

And the window was open.

Queen Maura, tenth ruler of Hasan Daeg and Empress of the Bhuttanian Empire, had escaped into the black and moonless night!

READ ON FOR A SPECIAL PREVIEW!
WALL OF GLORY
The Princess Maura Tales
Book 3

1

Maura rushed to meet KiKu by the east wall.

As a child, she had covered every inch of the city with the Dinii, memorizing every sewer hole, forgotten gate, and musty stairway in the garden city.

They planned to leave the city through an old caravan gate originally built for the Sivans that had not been used for centuries.

KiKu winced when he saw her. "Great Mother, your face is falling to your feet," he complained, watching her flesh drop to the ground.

"Just a piece here, a piece there," Maura mocked.

The alarm on KiKu's face did not vanish.

"It looks worse than it is," she said, trying to comfort him.

"You are injured! We cannot travel with you like that," KiKu insisted. He was not one to panic, but the empress' injuries were most unfortunate and ill-timed. He looked about, searching for a place to hide.

The city was being torn apart in the hunt for her. At any moment, the Bhuttanians could stumble upon them.

Maura pushed the tall man aside and mounted a Bhuttanian warhorse. "Listen, KiKu," she said. "Listen to the sound of a city being destroyed. It is all a ploy. I was meant to escape."

She donned the helmet that was hanging on the saddle horn. "How many people are going to die tonight because Dorak wants the Mother Bogazkoy? Hundreds? Thousands?" She paused, looking at the city. "Do you know what I did, KiKu? I had my women cut off the manhood from Dorak's men. I did some myself."

She pointed to her face. "This is not my blood. My blood is blue, not red. This is the blood of Bhuttanian men who stood between me and freedom. I needed a disguise to escape the palace, and those faceless men provided me one. I now know the true meaning of ruling. It is rule or be ruled. Kill or be killed."

Maura lowered the visor on her helmet and slapped the horse with the end of her reins.

The stallion whinnied and galloped off, aware that an unyielding hand controlled it.

KiKu jumped on his horse, wondering if the woman he followed had become worse than the aga he had betrayed.

2

They rode all night.

When chancing upon any Bhuttanian search parties, KiKu spoke for them, saying they had been on leave in O Konya and were now returning to their garrison in Qatou.

If any soldier questioned the blood on KiKu's partner's clothes, he would answer that O Konya was under martial law, and they had helped detain many citizens before leaving for their garrison.

Each time the bands of soldiers would let them pass, not realizing that the tall Bhuttanians were the empress and Zoar's former spylord.

Before dawn, KiKu led them to a small cave on a ridge just big enough to conceal them and their mounts. Two fresh mounts waited inside with needed provisions.

Maura jumped off her horse and collapsed on a bedroll that KiKu provided her. She was exhausted both physically and mentally.

KiKu handed Maura hardtack and a cup of water. "There will be no fire tonight," KiKu apologized. "Sorry about the rations but I had only a few hours to arrange this little escape of yours."

Maura grunted in agreement. "It is good that your cohorts can move so quickly and easily." She pondered for a moment.

"Getting these warhorses was no small task. How many Bhuttanians still work for you, KiKu?"

KiKu blinked while leaning against a rock munching on some hardtack. "The beauty of my system, Great Mother, is that if caught, you will never have any information to divulge to Dorak that could threaten my loyal followers."

She chortled. "In other words the less I know, the better."

"Correct, Great Mother."

"What do you get out of this if I win?"

"Your mother promised me my kingdom. I wish to gather my people if there are any left."

"My mother's wish is now my command, KiKu. I swear to you that if we prevail, you will have your kingdom."

"Upon your oath as Great Mother?"

"Upon my oath as Empress Maura de Magela."

"Then indeed we shall prevail." KiKu swallowed some water and rested his head on his chest.

Thinking KiKu had fallen asleep, Maura got up to care for the horses.

KiKu stuck his foot out and shook his head while still resting his closed eyes. "I will see to the horses in a moment, Great Mother. You must sleep."

Maura gratefully returned to her bedroll and was dreaming before her head came to rest.

3

Maura awoke the next afternoon.

She found KiKu squatting before the entrance of the cave surveying the valley below. "Any sign of trouble?" she asked, rubbing her sore muscles.

KiKu shook his head slightly. "Search parties were down in the valley. They have left to go on to Qatou, I suppose." He looked at Maura intently. "Your face doesn't look any better," he commented.

She felt her features with her hands as there was no mirror. "Some of the cuts are starting to get infected," she said. "I feel feverish."

"Can you do anything about it?" KiKu asked.

Maura shrugged her shoulders. "I guess I could heal myself before we leave tonight."

"Great Mother, may I suggest that if you can do so, you do it now. We may have to flee at any moment, and it would not do to have a sick woman on my hands."

Maura rubbed her face and did not answer KiKu.

"Great Mother, I know you are feeling sad about the death of Lady Sari, but being a ruler sometimes involves knowing when not to put your servants in needless danger."

Maura flinched at the mention of Sari and began to silently weep. "You know about Sari?"

"Before you came to the wall, one of my contacts made a brief visit. She told me that an imposter posing as you had committed suicide rather than be taken. I guessed that it was Lady Sari."

"And my guards?"

"It is correct that you cry for them. It shows that you still have a heart, and you honor them with your tears."

"If I had a heart, I would not have let them die."

"What else was to be done? You had to flee the city, and they willingly gave their lives to ensure that you could. They knew what they were doing. It is our way."

Maura gave KiKu a long, hard look. "Who?"

"Those who serve, Great Mother. We know our lives are expendable, and we accept our lot in life." His expression was one of acceptance and regret.

Maura left KiKu with his memories and moved to the back of the cave where she relieved herself. When finished, she perched upon a rock in the cave and began healing her face.

KiKu did not watch but gazed upon the valley, watching a hawk soar in the sky. If he could have escaped being spotted, KiKu would have contacted the hawk to take a message to the Dinii, but it was too much of a risk to call out.

An hour later, Maura jumped down from the rock and washed her face from a small tin of water. "How do I look?" she asked KiKu.

He studied her face, looking for marks or cuts. "You look like a young woman again, but you have the blue face of a de Magela."

KiKu walked to the opposite side of her, again studying her face. "I have heard of your regenerative powers, but this is the first time I have witnessed them for myself. It is truly amazing," he complimented. "Have you still the fever?"

"See for yourself."

KiKu cautiously extended his hand and touched her brow. "Dry and cool. No fever," he pronounced happily. "We will be able to travel tonight."

Maura nodded in agreement. "Where do we go from here?"

"We will travel south to Siva. There we will pose as a merchant with his obedient and humble wife."

"Are you going to pose as the wife?"

KiKu smiled a toothy grin.

For the first time, Maura noticed that KiKu was a good-looking man and not as old as she had believed. She wondered if he had a wife stashed somewhere. "Why don't we head north to the City of the Peaks?"

KiKu's smile vanished.

Alarmed, Maura grabbed his arm. "Why do you look like that? What has happened?"

KiKu bowed his head. He did not want to see her face as he told her. "The City of the Peaks is no more. Burned out."

"How?" cried Maura. "The city is impregnable!"

"Magic," was KiKu's simple reply.

"The Black Cacodemon!" Maura spat on the ground. Her face contorted as though she were struggling to find the right words. "What of the royal family—Empress Gitar and her children?" she asked quietly.

"I don't know. I suppose some got out."

"Why?" Maura felt as though someone had gutted her with a knife.

KiKu rubbed his unshaven face. "Dorak did not want the Dinii to help you if you fled. He put them on the run. I think you are right in that this is a trick. Soldiers should have been swarming over that west wall.

We did not see any until the road patrols. Easy enough to fool them. I think the hitch in their plans was that your disguise was too good. You threw them off, and now they've got to find you."

"In order to follow us!"

"Correct," KiKu said. His respect for the girl had increased. She was not stupid and, judging from her masquerade, was resourceful as well as ruthless. He had not recognized her at all when she first approached, and he was a master of disguises. "Dorak wants the Mother Bogazkoy."

"She will not accept him. He is not suitable for her purposes."

"Perhaps he doesn't know that or he doesn't believe it. Perhaps the Black Cacodemon has promised him the mating will work."

"Perhaps, perhaps. I need facts. I need to know who is left of the Dinii. I need to know where my western army is. You are supposed to be my spylord. Tell me something of value," she prodded in frustration.

"No one has seen the Dinii since the attack. We do not know where they have gone. They could have left the country."

"No," challenged Maura. "Chaun Maaun would never have left me. Never!"

"Chaun Maaun could be no longer, and you did

marry someone else."

Maura's face drained of color. She looked almost pale. "I was forced into marriage!"

KiKu gave her a look that clearly challenged the veracity of this last statement.

Maura buried her face in her warhorse's long mane, weeping. "That's a lie. I wanted to marry Dorak." Tears ran down her cheeks as shame illuminated her face.

The spy was moved to pity her. "We cannot help with whom we fall in love."

"But I loved Chaun Maaun and hated Dorak, at least in the beginning."

"Who knows the will of the heart? It can love many people in many ways. It can also hate and love at the same time. Zoar loved my sister, but he let her die in a hunting accident. Dorak both loved and hated his father, and yet he murdered him."

Maura wiped her tears away. "Dorak killed Zoar?"

KiKu nodded solemnly.

The horse that Maura was leaning on shifted and nuzzled her arm with his nose. "I don't know why, but that news makes me feel better."

"Misery abides company?"

"It explains Dorak's suffering." Maura scratched behind the ears of the contented horse. "I am glad that he suffers as I do."

"I think Dorak suffers a great deal. If he had been born with better parents, such as mine, he would have been a great man."

"Like you?"

KiKu ignored her sarcasm. "Dorak has the seeds of greatness within him, but with Zoar as his father, he didn't have a chance to become a man without being twisted in some fashion. Dorak was right to kill him."

"Who am I to judge Dorak when I allowed my beloved Sari to be killed?"

"You still do not realize."

"What?"

"Dorak is not the man to fear, nor the Black Cacodemon. It is Alexanee who must be watched."

"Why him?"

"Dorak will make a mistake that will cost him his life because he is impetuous." KiKu picked up some pebbles and flipped them back and forth between his fingers. "Like Dorak, the Black Cacodemon must be dealt with, but he is not invincible. His fatal defect is his ambition.

"Sooner or later, a spell will backfire or Dorak will tire of him and do the bastard in with a simple thrust of a sword. They are capable but flawed men who will perish from miscalculations."

KiKu put a pebble in his mouth and began to suck

on it. "Alexanee is different," he continued after he spat out the small stone. "He has no weaknesses. He does not gamble. He stays away from women. He is not a religious fanatic. Alexanee is highly intelligent, a brilliant strategist, even better than Zoar in his heyday. He is a man of moderation, both spiritually and emotionally."

Maura was intrigued by KiKu's analysis of Alexanee. She had never given him much thought. "It does not matter what attributes Alexanee has. He can never be aga."

"You are wrong about that, Great Mother. Only three people stand between Alexanee and his gaining control of the Bhuttanian Empire. Dorak, Jezra's son, and you."

KiKu lowered his voice. "Alexanee is Zoar's first child, born on the wrong side of the blanket you might say. His mother was a Bhuttanian noblewoman who was much older than Zoar. The details of Alexanee's birth remained quiet but when his mother died, Zoar brought Alexanee to court to serve as an officer in his army. Since Alexanee's parentage was not known, Zoar spared his life when killing the rest of his sons in favor of Dorak."

"Does he know?"

"Neither Dorak nor Alexanee know. I became privy to this information when Zoar and I were watching

Alexanee train once. Zoar said, 'There goes the best one of the lot, and I can't acknowledge him.'"

"And then you did some digging on your own?"

"Yes."

Maura remained silent while stroking the horse.

KiKu realized she did not wish to talk further. The hetmaan spent the remainder of the day resting near the mouth of the cave, though deep sleep eluded him. Noticing that he could no longer see the sun, KiKu looked outside. It was growing dark, and soon it would be safe for them to leave. He began saddling the horses.

Maura, who had been resting quietly on her bedroll, fell into step with KiKu to help with the horses and gather their gear. When finished, KiKu told the young empress to wait outside with their new mounts.

The young queen looked sad for she knew the fate of the two still-exhausted horses they had ridden from O Konya.

KiKu could not let them roam loose as their discovery would give away the direction of their escape.

Maura took the reins of the fresh mounts and walked a bit from the cave. She held her breath waiting for a panicked whinny or scream but heard nothing.

KiKu soon joined her, sheathing his knife. Taking his reins and a hank of mane, the lithe man pulled himself on the great warhorse. "I have killed many a man, but I can't abide hurting an animal." He put on his helmet. "Don't you think that is strange?" Without waiting for an answer, he kicked his horse and started down the mountain.

Maura followed behind him, ever alert for trouble.

They had traveled several miles when Maura heard a rustling in a nearby tree and looked up, her hand upon her sword.

Yeti sat upon a limb calmly eating a hedgepear. She looked happily at Maura and waved, "Greetings, Great Mother. I have been sent to fetch you!"

4

Y eti took another bite.

"Yeti!" exclaimed Maura as she turned her massive horse around. She jumped down and tied the horse securely to a low branch.

Yeti threw away her pear and glided down gracefully. Standing in the moonlight, she towered over Maura. She fluttered her massive wings in greeting and smiled a wide, sloppy grin.

The horse shied nervously, but Yeti spoke to it soothingly and patted its roan neck.

The stallion quickly settled down and began munching on grass.

Maura asked excitedly, "How did you find me?" She grabbed Yeti's hand and squeezed it with genuine affection.

"We heard that you had escaped. Iegani sent us out

to find you and take you to the Forbidden Zone."

"I am ready now."

Yeti held up her hand. "You cannot travel with me. It is too dangerous. I can only guide you."

"I don't understand," Maura said, her heart sinking.

"It is the Black Cacodemon," said KiKu, steadying his horse.

"Greetings, Hetmaan of Queen Maura," Yeti said, her wings fluttering.

KiKu noticed that the Dini did not refer to Maura as empress.

"You know his face?" asked Maura incredulously. "The identity of the hetmaan should be known only to a certain few."

"It is the first time I have seen him, but the Dinii know of the lord who worked as a double agent for Queen Abisola. Otherwise, how could I have rendez-voused with you in the meadow for our last meeting? He sends messages to us via the gootee." Yeti bowed in respect. "A master of disguises. I almost mistook you both for Bhuttanian soldiers and was going to kill you, but then I saw you were not Bhuttanian."

KiKu raised his eyebrows. "How is that?"

"Bhuttanians ride with their knees higher and heels turned downward. You ride with your feet level."

Yeti turned toward Maura. "You ride well, but you

look uncomfortable, as though you are not used to handling such a big animal. Nothing I could see directly. Just what I felt when I saw you riding."

"Lady, you are most observant. I could use someone like you. Would you like to be a spy?"

Yeti laughed easily. "I don't think I could easily blend in with the common folk."

KiKu jumped down off his horse and joined Yeti and Maura. He handed Yeti a waterskin from which she drank sparingly, due more to good manners than lack of thirst.

"I heard you say that you were sent here to fetch the empress," KiKu commented.

Yeti handed the waterskin back to him and nodded. "You are headed toward the border of Siva. There are bounty hunters and bandits waiting for you to cross."

KiKu whistled. This was a mighty blow to his plans. "Is there a reward?"

"Yes, but not from the Royal House of the Aga. It is offered by Baroness Mikkotto. She has put up the money."

"Mikkotto!" Maura ranted. "That murderous bitch."

Yeti, undisturbed by Maura's ire, continued, "The baroness has resettled on her estates with impunity. Other than answering to Dorak, she fears no one and is a law unto herself. Her estate is guarded by Hasan

Daegians loyal to her cause and Bhuttanians who serve as mercenaries."

Maura seemed stunned and wove a bit on her feet as though she were about to faint. She rubbed her forehead. "That would mean Dorak gave her permission to resettle. It means my parents' death by Mikkotto's plot was a ruse. He was going to kill them anyway, and he used her as a tool."

"It would seem so," replied Yeti, thinking kindly of Abisola and Iasos. They had been worthy rulers, and she was sorry they were gone.

Maura cast a wicked eye upon KiKu. "Did you know of this?"

KiKu shook his head and looked questioningly at Yeti. "None of my sources have mentioned Mikkotto since last spring. I find this information surprising."

Maura slapped KiKu hard across the face, almost knocking him off his feet. "You had better not be lying to me. If you fail me again, I will kill you."

KiKu's face remained hard and impassive, but it was evident that he was struggling to control himself. He took off his corselet of chainmail and dropped it on the ground, then put his hand on his sword.

Yeti stepped forward, but Maura grabbed her arm.

KiKu unsheathed his sword and presented its hilt to Maura.

She took it.

"I have offended thee. I am dishonored. Take my life so that I may die with honor, or permit me to die by my own hand," he begged.

"I will neither kill you nor grant permission to die by suicide," said Maura coldly. "You have treated me like a child since we met. I will forgive you since I have indeed acted as a child who could not see beyond her nose. But now I am truly the Ruling Lady of Hasan Daeg. Do you know why?"

Maura tapped on her chest as she spoke. "Because in here, there is no more a child, only a queen who needs your help getting to the Mother Bogazkoy so she may fulfill her destiny." She pointed the sword to the ground. "Pledge your allegiance to me."

KiKu fell to his knees, his face red with shame that he had failed his sovereign. He prostrated himself before Maura. "I pledge with my life and honor that I will live to obey you in all things and to serve the House of de Magela."

Maura asked, "Upon your life?"

"Upon my life!"

"Rise then and serve me well. We will never discuss this again."

KiKu rose from the ground and dusted off his clothes. He seemed genuinely chastised.

Yeti wondered if she would eventually have to kill him to protect Maura. It would be a pity as KiKu was such a valuable resource.

She sauntered over to a kokobo tree and pulled a small pouch from a knothole, handing it to Maura. "You are not to go by land to Siva. You are to go to the Sacred Lake of Yappor. There the Lahorians will take care of you."

"The Lahorians again," scoffed Maura, opening the pouch. She handed the contents to KiKu who held them up to the moonlight so all could see.

Yeti waved him away. "I can see in the dark without light," she said.

Inside the pouch was a map drawn on leather with berry juice. Maura was surprised and looked at Yeti. "Did you do this?"

Yeti smiled. "I can also read and write. Empress Gitar decided everyone needed to read, so we all learned. Badly at first, but better as time goes on."

She fingered the outlines on the map. "Here is an old hunter's trail that you will take to the Sacred Lake. From there the Lahorians will transport you and KiKu to the Forbidden Zone."

The hairs on the back of Maura's neck stood up at the mention of the Forbidden Zone, a place not visited by any Hasan Daegian since prohibited by Mekonia, their nature goddess.

"Why can't you fly the empress to the lake?" asked KiKu.

"Is empress your title now?" asked Yeti.

Maura lowered her eyes. "There is only one empress, and she is Gitar."

"Yes, that is what she thinks. She would want me to remind you," Yeti replied.

Peering at the map, KiKu asked again, "Why can't you transport her to the lake?"

Yeti lowered her head to study the bald man. "Because you will have a better chance of making it if you remain disguised as Bhuttanians. There is too great a risk that we would be shot out of the sky. The Bhuttanians have been ordered to shoot anything larger than an eagle flying. I can only travel when the sky is pitch black. There is a full moon tonight. We would make an easy target."

"Makes sense," said KiKu as he folded the map. He seemed to have forgotten the unsettling reprimand he had received only moments before.

"What of Gitar and Chaun Maaun?" asked Maura, her heart slowing down to take the shock of any bad news.

"I cannot tell you where they are, but they are alive," Yeti replied, her face lined with sadness. "Empress

Gitar has aged with grief. All her daughters were killed when the Black Cacodemon destroyed the city."

Maura groaned.

"Chaun Maaun lives. He never leaves his mother's side." Yeti handed the pouch to KiKu, who placed the map carefully inside his tunic. "He wants to see you, Maura."

Maura's eyes widened with apprehension. "Where?"

"He would not say. He wanted me only to tell you that he will see you but at his discretion."

Maura's heart raced as her eyes took on a strange light.

Yeti placed her hand on Maura's shoulder.

"Don't expect too much, little sparrow. He has changed and is not the same Chaun Maaun that you knew before. It has been terrible for him. He lives now only to hate the Bhuttanians. He is consumed with it."

"Does he wish to harm our queen?" KiKu asked, wondering how he was going to subdue a Dini. Without waiting for an answer, KiKu pleaded with Maura, "You must not see him."

Maura shamelessly brushed a tear from her cheek. "Tell Chaun Maaun I will see him on his conditions."

"You must not!" KiKu reiterated. "If he is that angry, he might try to kill you." KiKu looked at Yeti for support.

None was forthcoming.

"I will give him the satisfaction of calling me a traitor."

KiKu said, "What if he tries to kill you? Not even you can fight a Dini!"

Maura whispered, "Do you think that is the worst thing he can do to me?"

Yeti grunted with approval.

KiKu was desperate. "Yeti, help me. Persuade her not to see Prince Chaun Maaun."

Yeti shrugged her shoulders. "Chaun Maaun was her betrothed. His love was as pure as the water in the Sacred Lake of Yappor. She betrayed him for a human who was a murderer and butcher of both Hasan Daegians and Dinii. Now he wants satisfaction. It is the Dinii way. Maura was raised with the Dinii. She will follow our customs in this matter."

"You knew about us?" asked Maura.

"Little sparrow, everyone knew. The young hide their love not well at all." Yeti looked at the night sky. "You must hurry now. Every minute counts. I will follow you when I can. If anyone comes after you, I will kill them. Remember—take the shortcut to the Sacred Lake of Yappor."

"What happens once we get there?" asked KiKu.

"Stand at the edge of the lake. They have been waiting for you and are keeping watch. Once you arrive, they will transport you to the Forbidden Zone. You must do as they say."

"Can they be trusted?" Maura asked.

Yeti smiled. "As much as an old enemy can be. Their survival depends upon you at the moment. They will keep you safe enough."

Maura hugged Yeti warmly, inhaling her musky scent.

Yeti rested her chin on the top of Maura's head and brought her wings around to encircle them. "You smell like a barn, Yeti," whispered Maura.

"That is what you have always said, little sparrow," cooed Yeti, embracing Maura with her powerful wings. Yeti gave her one last tight squeeze before retracting her wings. "You must go now. Be careful." Yeti cuffed Maura under the chin.

"Chaun Maaun?"

"I will tell him that you will meet with him. Now go!"

Maura jumped onto her horse and sped off, following KiKu.

Yeti watched them until they disappeared deep into the forest and then flew back to her hiding place in the tree.

Tarsus handed her another hedgepear. "She looks

good for having gone through so much."

"The young always recover fast."

"That was a very inventive lie about Mikkotto and Dorak," Tarsus commented.

"It is Iegani's doing, not mine. It's his dirty business." Yeti threw the fruit away in disgust.

"Will Iegani let her see Chaun Maaun?"

Yeti wiped her mouth with her forearm. "Not even Iegani can control the prince. Chaun Maaun will have his way eventually."

Tarsus grunted and leaned back against a limb, quickly falling asleep.

Yeti watched the moon. She felt deeply for the woman she held as a baby and guarded. She remembered the times she had picked up the child who gurgled and laughed as she pulled on Yeti's feathers. Yeti felt a stirring in her heart that she did not understand but accepted.

She loved the girl and felt Iegani was wrong to deceive her. Nothing good would come of it. Sooner or later, it would catch up with him. Hopefully, Yeti would be far away when that happened.

Other Books By Abigail Keam

Princess Maura Tales

Josiah Reynolds Mysteries

Last Chance For Love Series

CHECK OUT THE
JOSIAH REYNOLDS MYSTERIES!

"Abigail Keam writes with vision and understanding."
Midwest Book Review

"We are introduced to a cast of characters and a storyline that, like honey, is sweet and delicious."
Linda Hinchcliff, Chevy Chase Magazine

"Ms. Keam writes such that readers want to know more of Josiah's life and the ending will not disappoint their need to know."
Readers' Favorite

About The Author

Hello, my friend. I hope you are enjoying the Princess Maura Tales. I had such fun writing about Princess Maura and her adventures. If you like to read in other genres, I also write *The Josiah Reynolds Mystery Series* and *The Last Chance For Love Series*, a happily-ever-after sweet romance series. I would love to hear from you.
abigailkeam@windstream.net

If you like my stories, please leave a review
and tell your friends about me.

www.abigailkeam.com